The Retreat

FINDING HIM

L.M. SOMERTON

Finding Him
ISBN # 978-1-83943-773-1
©Copyright L.M. Somerton 2022
Cover Art by Fiona Jayde ©Copyright March 2022
Interior text design by Claire Siemaszkiewicz
Pride Publishing

Pride Publishing books by L.M. Somerton

Single Books
Mountain Rescue
Black Dog
The Portrait
Stroke Rate
Chemical Bonds
Testing Lysander
Owned by the Sea

The Wyverns
Mantrap
Deathtrap
Rattrap
Sand Trap
Steel Trap

Tales from The Edge
Reaching the Edge
Living on the Edge
Dancing on the Edge
A Double-Edged Sword
Rough Around the Edges
Scorched Edges
Driven to the Edge
Binding the Edges
Edging Closer

Investigating Love
Rasputin's Kiss
Evil's Embrace
Tarot's Love

Warlocks
Elemental Love
Elemental Hope
Elemental Faith

The Retreat
Serving Him
Trusting Him
Finding Him

Fairground Attractions
Ghost Train
Merry-Go-Round
Helter Skelter

Treasure Trove Antiques
The Lucky Cat
The Gilded Mirror

Anthologies
Racing Hearts: Keeping the Luck
His Rules: Tagging Mackenzie
Hard Evidence: Secret's Hold

FINDING HIM

Dedication

To finding *the one*.

Chapter One

Carey Hoffman stepped out of the air-conditioned limousine into the burning heat of a Palm Springs summer's day. The air shimmered, and he half-expected to see a mirage in the distance along with a camel train and a bunch of wandering nomads. The sun's intensity made the greenery around him all the more astounding. Extensive, manicured lawns stretched to either side of the sweeping drive and in front of him stood the biggest, most palatial house he'd ever seen. He could only imagine how much watering all that lush grass would need.

"It's enormous." Pure white, the sun reflecting off the building's curved walls was blinding. Carey slipped on his sunglasses to reduce the combined glare of the sun and the paintwork. He couldn't decide whether he liked the property or not. There was no doubt that it was extravagant and no question it was unique. "Probably designed by some celebrity architect for an extortionate fee," Carey muttered. "It must be worth a small fortune."

"I kind of like the smooth lines, it's all curves, no harsh edges." Alistair, Carey's partner and submissive, joined him, slipping his hand into Carey's. "It doesn't come across as ostentatious as the McMansions you see in California. It's understated, restrained somehow."

"That's your artistic eye at work, love. There's way too much white for my liking. What's wrong with a bit of color? Or at the very least a shade of white that isn't…misty cloud or curdled milk or something. There are whole pages of so-called whites on paint charts, though they mostly look the same to me."

Alistair gave him a gentle smile. "The heat's getting to you, isn't it, Sir?"

"How do people around here not combust? This place is like a furnace—I feel like I'm desiccating just standing here. What I wouldn't give for a dose of London drizzle right now and that's not something I ever thought I'd say."

"We're English. Our bodies are not equipped for more than two hot days a year—and by hot, I mean low eighties, not high nineties. Everything here seems to be air-conditioned to the point of frigidity, and I'm sure the house will be, too, once we get inside. You'll be much happier then."

"It's entirely your fault we're here, you know that? Now you're a famous photographer, everyone wants a piece of you. Even multimillionaires. A personal invite from Taylor Denman is not to be sniffed at." Carey gave Alistair a kiss to demonstrate his pride. "I'm so proud of you love, even if I am being fried alive."

"Do you wish I'd turned down the invitation?" Alistair gazed at him anxiously. "I would have if you'd asked me to."

"Absolutely not! Ignore me, sweetheart. The heat's making me fractious. I'm very glad you accepted the invitation and I'm intrigued to meet Mr. Denman since he sponsored your exhibition in San Francisco. It was an enormous success. I've never seen so many sold stickers at a show before and it wouldn't surprise me if he bought some of the pictures himself. You worked really hard to get everything set up, the launch was wonderful but exhausting. Mr. Denman's offer to spend a few days at one of his hotels was a perfect way to end our trip so you could hardly turn down an invitation to meet him in person. It's a small price to pay for an all-expenses paid stay in the best hotel in Palm Springs."

They walked toward the house, glittering quartz gravel crunching beneath their shoes.

"I have to confess I'm a little nervous." Alistair gripped Carey's hand tighter.

"There's no need to be. I'm here and I'll take care of you."

"You always do." Alistair smiled, and Carey's breath hitched. Alistair was beautiful, the sun glinting on his blond hair, his skin showing a hint of tan from several weeks in the sun.

"And I always will." There was no doubt about that in Carey's mind. Taking care of Alistair was the single most fulfilling part of his existence.

As they approached the huge front door of the property, it swung open. Carey expected to see a butler or maybe a personal assistant, but it was Taylor Denman himself who stood waiting for them. Carey recognized him from pictures he'd seen in the press. Taylor was casually dressed in jeans and a light blue shirt, the sleeves rolled up to reveal tanned arms and the curl of a tattoo. He was a striking man, about Carey's age, his chestnut hair starting to silver at the temples. A trace of stubble shaded his jaw, and there were laughter lines around his eyes.

"Welcome, gentlemen. I'm so glad you were able to make the trip from San Francisco." Taylor stepped forward with a welcoming smile.

"Thank you for inviting us, Mr. Denman," Alistair said. "We're so happy to meet you."

"Call me Taylor. You're Alistair of course, I know you from your catalog picture, so this must be Carey." He shook hands with Carey first, then with Alistair. "Come inside, it's hotter than the surface of the fucking sun out here, excuse my language."

Alistair giggled. "You and Carey are going to get along really well."

"I thought it was only us rain-soaked Brits who couldn't handle it," Carey said, following Taylor into the icy-cool interior of his home. "I'm melting."

"I was born in Canada. Alberta. I don't think I'll ever get used to the heat, but my business interests make having a home here convenient. I keep an apartment in New York but I thought you'd appreciate a few days here in Palm Springs after the bustle of San Francisco. It's a lot more relaxing than The Big Apple."

"We certainly appreciate it," Carey said, gazing around the entrance hall. "It's rare that we get to spend a few days alone together, and the exhibition was a little frantic. Thanks to you it drew a lot of attention." He was impressed by the cool colors and sleek minimalist design. The area managed to be welcoming even though the cathedral-like ceiling height could have made it intimidating.

His eye was drawn to a wall displaying a single large picture. Carey smiled. It was one of Alistair's photographs, blown up to huge proportions. The original was one of Carey's favorites. It showed a vast, ancient oak, standing alone in a rural landscape at twilight, its gnarled limbs outlined against the sky. A silhouette of a fox was just visible at its base. Ironically, it hadn't taken hours of patient waiting for an animal to appear. He and Alistair had driven out to the Chiltern hills one afternoon and had been taking a stroll after an early dinner at a nearby restaurant. Alistair, his photographer's instinct always active, had lifted his camera and taken the snap after spotting movement. He hadn't even known it was a fox until he'd looked at the digital image. It had been pure luck that the picture had come out so well. It had sold at a London gallery, but the buyer had remained anonymous.

Alistair edged a little closer to Carey's side, blushing. "Now you know what happened to the picture," Carey said with a chuckle.

"I was curious," Alistair admitted. "Anonymous buyers are intriguing."

"The original is in my study," Taylor said. "I had this print made specifically for this space, and you have no idea how many compliments it draws. I'm loath to praise your work in public, Alistair because it never fails to increase competition for the pictures I want to buy. I'm a covetous man—I want the best for myself."

"I'm so flattered. The picture certainly suits this space. I'm glad it went to someone who appreciates it."

"Well, I've added several more to my collection thanks to the San Francisco exhibition. Shameless self-interest got me involved and as sponsor I got first pick, which caused huge annoyance to several acquaintances. An added bonus, I admit." He grinned, mischief glittering in his eyes. "But I have to confess that it's not the reason I've invited you both here. I'm afraid I have been somewhat dishonest. Of course, I sponsored the exhibition for absolutely genuine reasons, but over the last year things have come to light that I think you may be able to help me with. A personal matter."

"You have my attention," Carey said. "Does this have something to do with Alistair's photography skills?"

"No. Actually, Carey, it's you that I think can help. Let's go sit in the sun room. I have light snacks set out in there, and cold drinks. We can relax and you can hear me out."

Carey exchanged a curious glance with Alastair who shrugged, apparently unconcerned by the mystery. They both followed Taylor through the house pausing to admire the pictures and sculptures that were displayed everywhere.

The sun room proved to be constructed entirely of glass but managed to remain ice-cold. Several comfortable loungers surrounded a low glass table and there was a magnificent view of the sweeping grounds. Carey guessed that the hint of glittering water in the distance must be a pool.

They settled into their seats, Carey and Alistair next to each other, Taylor opposite them. Taylor offered them a selection of drinks. Alistair opted for chilled mango juice while Carey accepted a light beer, mirroring Taylor's choice. On the table sat several platters of cold finger food, which was tempting but

Carey wanted to hear what Taylor had to say before switching his attention to snacks.

"How do I start?" Taylor leaned forward, steepling his fingers.

"I find it's always best to be direct," Carey said.

"Perhaps the best way for me to introduce this subject is to mention that we have a mutual acquaintance." Taylor stared at the view rather than meeting Carey's eyes. "A close friend of mine, Lorcan Wilder."

Alistair reached for Carey's hand. Carey took it and gave it a comforting squeeze. "Lorcan is a good friend of mine too. How do you know him?"

"We met through various business dealings before he sold his company, and now I'm involved in some of his philanthropic endeavors. I contribute to a number of the projects he supports through his foundation but that's not why I mentioned his name. Lorcan told me all about his stay at The Retreat and how he met his Rowan, who I have to say is the sweetest young man. He's perfect for Lorcan."

"They are very well suited," Carey said, not bothering to conceal his curiosity. "But what's your interest in The Retreat? I have to admit I would never have guessed that was what you wanted to talk about."

"I know I can trust your discretion," Taylor said, finally meeting Carey's gaze. "And for that reason I'm going to give you a bit of context. My wife died a long time ago, but she and I enjoyed a relationship that was not always vanilla. I'm not completely ignorant of the BDSM lifestyle, though Anya and I never played outside of the privacy of our own home. I've also known Lorcan for a long time, he knows I like to play occasionally."

"You understand that The Retreat only caters for men?" Carey said.

"Yes, I do." Taylor chuckled. "I'm sorry, I'm usually more direct than this. I'm not interested in a stay at The Retreat for myself. It's for my son, Zac."

Alistair squeezed Carey's fingers, and Carey gave him a nod to let him know he could speak. "Mr. Denman, Taylor, are you saying you want to book a stay at a BDSM retreat for your son?"

"I suppose I am, Alistair."

"Forgive me for saying so, but that's rather unusual."

"I realize it's rather a strange request, but I can assure you it's in his best interests."

"That's so cool." Alistair beamed. "The Retreat is an amazing place."

"We are a little biased, though," Carey admitted. "Okay, a lot biased."

"I can assure you that Lorcan has the same opinion otherwise we wouldn't be talking. I've taken his advice on this. I know this is...unusual but I'm extremely fortunate in having a very close relationship with Zac. He's always been very open with me, and I'm proud that he feels able to be that way. I'm not sure whether I knew he was gay before he did or if it was the other way round, but he never had to come out to me. I've always been as supportive as possible and encouraged him to be open when he felt he could." Carey nodded his approval. "However, being my son comes with a unique set of issues. Over the years there have been several threats against Zac. Let me be clear, that's got nothing to do with his sexuality, it's to do with my money and the fact that he's my only heir. Zac has always had to deal with understanding that he's at risk of being kidnapped. He's recently finished college but his roommate was also his bodyguard. Other than the Internet, he's had very little chance to explore the way he tells me he feels."

"And how is that? Does he think he's a Dom?" Carey asked.

Taylor shook his head. "The opposite. He takes after his mother. He has her looks and her submissive streak. He tells me that he wants to explore that further. He's an adult, he can do as he pleases but he wants my blessing, and I want him safe."

"Forgive me," Carey said, "I'm still not quite seeing what you need from us."

"It's not my intention to be obtuse. I want to help Zac find a Dom in a safe, protected environment. He can't go to clubs or leather bars—he'd be recognized. Don't get me wrong, I have no issue with reputation here, though Zac deserves his privacy. It's a security problem. I want him to have the opportunity to experience submission and potentially meet someone he can connect with in the same profound way that I did with his mother. The catch is that longer term, his Dom will also need to be his protector. I need a good man to keep my boy safe, Carey. That's what I want you to help me with, though I don't expect a short stay at The Retreat to solve everything of course—just get Zac on the start line as it were."

Alistair sighed. "That's so amazing. Zac is very lucky to have such good relationship with you."

"Alistair's relationship with his father was nowhere near so healthy," Carey said, repressing a shudder at the memory of the evil that man had committed. "But you realize, Taylor, that I can't countenance going anywhere with this unless it's with Zac's full agreement."

"Of course, and that's why I'd like you to meet him. He's fully on board with the plan, I can assure you. You can come in now, Zac."

Carey hadn't noticed the door that Zac came through, until it opened, it was so cleverly concealed in a mirrored panel. The young man that strolled across the room to join them was visually striking and clearly Taylor's son. His wavy hair was a shade darker than his father's, his cheekbones were sharper and his lips fuller. It was his eyes that caught Carey's attention. The unusual shade of pale green, framed by dark lashes, was arresting. Zac's mother must have been an exceptionally attractive woman.

"Zac, come and meet Mr. Hoffman and his famous photographer partner, Alistair. I need you to convince Mr. Hoffman that I'm not trying to pimp you out," Taylor said, rising to give his son a hug.

"You're not?" Zac grinned as they pulled apart and laughed when Taylor gave him a light cuff. "Okay, you're not!" He turned to Carey. "It's a pleasure to meet you, Mr. Hoffman. My friend Rowan thinks you have magical powers when it comes to matchmaking." Zac's voice was deep and melodic. He spoke with quiet confidence, but Carey could tell he was nervous.

"It's a pleasure to meet you, Zac. This is my...partner, Alistair," Carey said.

Alistair rolled his eyes. He pulled his shirt down to show the narrow leather collar around his neck. "I'm his *submissive* partner. If you're friends with Rowan, then I guess you understand how that works."

"It's a great pleasure, Alistair. Dad moons over your pictures constantly. He's quite the fan boy."

"Zac!" Taylor protested, "Stop giving away my secrets."

Alistair blushed. "I'm a bit in awe. Can we get back to talking about submission—it's a much easier topic?"

Carey gave Alistair a fond look. "So, you're hoping to learn more about the lifestyle, Zac?"

"I want to. I know this whole plan must seem crazy but...well, it *is* kind of crazy, I suppose. I want to find out what sort of submissive I am. I want to meet different men in a way that doesn't send my dad into a tailspin. When Lorcan told us about The Retreat, everything fell into place, and it seemed like the perfect solution."

"We don't run a dating agency," Carey said. "What we can do is provide Dominants for you to play with, different men with differing skill sets depending on what you think you might like to try. Are you a masochist? Do you enjoy pain? Do you want to be humiliated or forced?"

"I don't know!" Zac's face pinked. "I just know I want to find out." He scuffed the toe of his sneaker against the polished floor. "Can you help me?"

"Of course we will!" Alistair jumped to his feet then pulled Zac into a hug. "Won't we, Sir?"

Carey knew there and then that he had no choice in the matter. "Something you'll soon realize, Zac, is that submissives hold all the power in our world." Carey shook his head.

Alistair giggled as he returned to Carey's side. "Well, we *will* help, won't we? You love a challenge, Sir."

"If you say so, love." Taylor seemed bemused, Zac hopeful. "There are details to be hammered out, but yes," Carey said. "The Retreat should be able to fulfill what you need to a certain extent. I can't guarantee you'll meet anyone you want to make a lasting connection with but I'll discuss your case with Luke Redding, the manager at The Retreat, and he'll be in touch. There's an extensive waiting list, so I don't know how long it will be before…"

"I made the reservation some time ago," Taylor said. "Under a false name. Zac and I decided to wait until he'd finished college, but we've been planning this for a while. The booking is for two weeks and begins at the start of September. I trust that will give you adequate time to prepare?"

Carey wasn't often surprised, and he didn't let it show on his face, but he was impressed by Taylor's forethought. He was also a little concerned about the timescale. "That will be fine. We'll look forward to welcoming Zac in September."

"Excellent. Now that's agreed, perhaps Zac could loan Alistair some swim shorts and show him the pool, while I take you to admire my wine cellar? I don't get the chance to show it off often enough, and Lorcan tells me you know your vintages. Now our business is done, it would be very nice to relax with new friends, if you don't mind staying a while."

Carey glanced at Alistair who was bouncing with excitement. "That sounds perfect." Alistair and Zac were already moving. "You can tell me all about Zac. Any insights you can give me will be helpful." Carey fancied that Taylor's smile was warmer, less tense, than before. "And I'm sure he'll give Alistair all kinds of useful information."

"I'll do my best, Carey, and perhaps you can help me choose an appropriate bottle to go with supper. My driver will take you back to your hotel this evening."

Carey relaxed. Good company, food and wine would be the perfect end to a surprising day. There would be time back in England to consider how best to meet Zac's unusual needs.

Chapter Two

After a week of unusually high temperatures for England in August, Luke Redding was glad that his office was less oven-like than it had been in recent days, especially as preparations for The Retreat's next guest had been getting a bit frantic. "Is everything ready?" Carey's low tones sounded from the speakerphone on Luke's desk. He frowned at his computer screen, glad that Carey hadn't made a video call and consequently couldn't see his expression. "We're set this end, Carey, but the situation is a little…unusual, even for The Retreat and that's saying something. A little longer to prepare wouldn't have gone amiss either."

Carey's deep chuckle filled the room. "As Alistair saw fit to remind me when we first spoke to Taylor Denman about all this, I do love a challenge and by default that means you do too. I can see you rolling your eyes by the way."

Luke glared at the phone. "Save those kind of insights for Alistair, Carey."

"We're good to go here too. I've made arrangements with the four men we've selected spread over Zac's two-week stay, with space to take stock between each visit. He'll have two days with each of them. Enough time to get a taste of some different species of Dom."

Luke shook his head before remembering Carey couldn't see him. "You make them sound like samples from a tasting menu."

"That's not far from the truth. As I told you, Zac has had a very sheltered, protected upbringing out of necessity. It's a miracle, and a testament to his father that he's turned out as well adjusted as he has. He wants to get a feel for different aspects of the lifestyle in a safe environment and if sparks fly with any of them, he's free to progress with that man if he wants to. All the Doms are very willing participants, and they know the score. They are also aware that they might not be needed at short notice. They've signed confidentiality agreements, though I trust them all — it's insurance that Taylor Denman required."

"They'll have the run of the place," Luke said. "I've reduced staffing to a bare minimum as you requested, so there will be me acting as dungeon master, Tor in the kitchen with, God help us all, Rayne helping him out alongside his driving duties. Skye will cover general housekeeping, but Zac knows he'll be responsible for any duties related to the equipment he uses. We'll all work around the requirements of the Doms. Everyone else has either been redeployed to The Underground or is taking some holiday."

"Excellent. I've taken a few measures to beef up security, which you know about. The camera system has had the latest upgrade, but I've also decided to send someone else your way. Dale Gastrell is a club member and old friend of mine. He has an interesting if vague history in the armed services but retired after taking a bullet to the hip that left him with a limp. He runs his own very successful landscaping company now, so he's going to work undercover as your gardener for the duration of Zac's stay."

"That name sounds familiar, though I don't think I've met him."

"Neither of you are frequent visitors to The Underground so it's not likely but I know quite a few members use his services so you may have heard his name mentioned."

"An extra pair of eyes around the place will be welcome," Luke said. "Especially someone trained to spot things that might be suspicious. Tor and I will be too busy to do much surveillance. Does Zac know about Dale?"

"No, and I think it's better it stays that way. Dale needs to blend into the background and be inconspicuous. Only you and I know why Dale will be there. To everyone else, he's a new gardener. He'll be with you tomorrow morning. There's no need to brief him about Zac, I've shared his file already."

"Fair enough. Anything else I need to know?"

"Taylor emailed to let me know Zac has a mild allergy to kiwi fruit—brings him out in hives apparently, so pass that on to Tor would you?"

Luke tapped a note into Zac's computer file. "Will do. Mr. Denman really does sanction all this then?"

"He's footing the bill. He's a nice guy, Luke. Looking out for his son in the best way he knows. Zac is no spoiled brat. His close relationship with Taylor has been instrumental in making him who he is — confident in most aspects of his life. His submission is something that needs a nudge is all. He embraces it, knows inherently that it's something he needs but he's had no way to explore those feelings. Taylor's a Dom, though he happily admits he's only played around the edges in the years since he lost his wife, so he understands Zac well."

"We'll do our best to give him the introduction to the lifestyle he's looking for." Luke leaned back in his chair. "I'll keep you updated as always, Carey."

"I don't doubt it. Good luck—not that you'll need it—and give my best to Skye, Tor and Rayne."

Luke said his goodbyes then brought up the file of the Dom who would be arriving two days after Zac. He already knew it inside out, but another refresher wouldn't be wasted. He'd been working for an hour when there was a soft knock at the door. His heart gave a little jump and he smiled. "Come in, Skye." The love of Luke's life, his submissive, Skye sidled around the door, barely opening it wide enough to get inside.

"Hello, Sir." Skye took three paces then sank to his knees next to Luke's chair. "I missed you."

Luke ruffled Skye's silver-gray hair. "I missed you too, as always. You're a little later back than I expected, sweetheart. Did Sue get away on time?" Professor Sue Doring was Skye's eccentric, scatty employer for part of the week. She fulfilled every known stereotype of an academic so buried in historical research that she forgot what century she was living in, so Luke had good cause to doubt her timeliness.

"She was running late, of course, because when isn't she? But I got her and her baggage into the taxi when it arrived. Lord knows what she packed — ski boots rather than a snorkel probably — but that's someone else's problem now. I'm all yours for the next two weeks, while she's diving wreck sites with her husband off Bali."

"You're all mine, all of the time." Luke wound a strand of Skye's hair around his finger then gave it a little tug. "Best you remember that."

"Yes, Sir." Skye beamed.

"Are you looking forward to our new guest arriving?"

"I am! Alistair called and told me Zac is really sweet. He's being so brave meeting four different Doms. I'd be scared out of my mind."

"Then it's a good job you don't need to meet any other Doms, isn't it?" Luke tried not to growl, but the idea of Skye being anywhere near another Dom made his skin itch. "And never will."

"It is. I love it when you get all growly and possessive." Skye stroked Luke's thigh then gave Luke's chair a push. It glided a few inches, giving Skye enough room to wiggle under his desk, where he knelt between Luke's knees, cheeky grin on his face.

"I remember when you were sweet and shy." Luke parted his legs wider.

"I'm only confident when I'm with you, Sir."

"I can work with that." Luke eyed his open office door, but Skye's parted lips and violet eyes were too much to resist. "I need to hone my willpower," Luke said to no one in particular.

Skye took that as permission to lower Luke's zipper. "Sir, I'm scandalized. Where's your underwear?" He released Luke's straining cock from the confines of his trousers. "Did you get distracted when you were dressing this morning?"

"Yes, by your cute behind if I recall correctly but Skye, unless you're visualizing a future in chastity, stop talking. There are far better uses for your mouth at this precise moment."

"Yes, Sir." Skye gave the head of Luke's cock a delicate lick. Just the flick of his tongue was enough to have Luke gripping the arms of his chair so hard his knuckles went white. Then Tor stuck his head around the office door, and Luke fought back a groan. He edged his chair forward a little, not daring to make eye contact with Skye who was shaking with suppressed laughter. *I am going to spank his behind so hard.* "Tor, what can I do for you? I thought you were up to your elbows in flour, baking bread for tomorrow."

"It's proving, so I have a few minutes. I wanted to check to see if there are any last-minute instructions for our next guest. Uh, you're a bit flushed. Are you feeling okay?"

"I'm good. It's a little warm in here."

"Not as bad as it has been, though, right? I hate heatwaves with a vengeance. We should investigate air conditioning."

"I'll make a note."

"So…Zac Denman?"

"He has a kiwi allergy, nothing else new. Rayne is collecting him from Farnborough Airport tomorrow morning—he's coming in on his father's private jet, so all being well he'll be with us by lunchtime."

"Sounds like a step up from cattle class on Ryanair. I have the list of his likes and dislikes. I have the first Dom's details too, so I'm set. Do I get any of Skye's time or are you going to keep him all to yourself?"

Skye planted a kiss on Luke's knee, and Luke sucked in a breath, his face heating.

"Are you sure you're okay? I could get you a painkiller or a glass of iced water…"

"I'm fine. Really."

"I could bring you a snack or something else to drink…"

"No! No, that's kind but I'll wait for dinner this evening." Luke tried to take slow, even breaths but Skye was doing wicked things with his tongue.

"Skye's due back soon, isn't he?"

"I believe so. He'll be at your disposal for any serving duties." Luke gave an involuntary twitch. Tor's eyes widened.

"Serving duties…yes, I see. I think I'll be leaving now."

"That would be best." Luke gave a pained sigh. "Stop grinning, Tor, or I will overcook scrambled eggs in your favorite skillet." A muffled snort came from beneath the desk.

"That's a low…blow…"

"Out! Get out!" Tor made a hasty exit, chortling as he went. "You are in a whole world of trouble, young man." Luke shoved his chair back.

"Can I be in trouble later, Sir? I've been at eye level with your dick for the last five minutes and it's so pretty. I want to taste…"

"Fine. I may as well enjoy the here and now because I'm going to be looking at Tor's smirking face over meals for the rest of my life."

"You know he's gonna tell Rayne."

"Oh God. That's all I need."

Skye scrambled closer, and Luke forgot all about the ribbing he was going to get later. *By the love of all that is holy…* Skye had absorbed every lesson Luke had given him in how to give a superlative blow job. He was utterly focused on Luke's pleasure, using his tongue to worship every sensitive spot on Luke's shaft. Skye's head bobbing up and down brought Luke so close to coming he had to squeeze his eyes shut. He took a few deep breaths, determined to enjoy the moment and not embarrass himself like a horny teenager but came to the conclusion that holding out for the sake of appearances was a waste of time. It would make Skye happy to know he'd made Luke lose control. He opened his eyes, grabbed Skye's hair and allowed his orgasm to roll through him. Skye sucked with renewed enthusiasm, taking Luke deep into his throat as he shot. Skye hummed as he swallowed, his eyes sparkling.

Luke gave himself a few moments before he released his grip on Skye's silver locks. Skye leaned back, letting Luke's shaft slip from his mouth. He licked his lips then gave Luke a smile that managed to be both sweet and wicked.

"That was so yummy, Sir."

"Your evening discipline is going to be gratifying," Luke muttered as Skye scrambled from beneath the desk. Luke zipped up then took a moment before attempting to stand. He didn't trust his legs to hold him.

"Would you like me to go make you a cup of tea, Sir?"

"Such an innocent phrase from that wicked mouth. Yes. Tea would be good. I'll come and join you in the staff dining room shortly."

Skye bounced from the room, energetic as a spring lamb, leaving Luke with a wry smile on his face. "I need to bottle that bounce. I'd make a fortune." He wasted a few minutes tidying some papers while he composed himself. There was no way he was going anywhere near Tor, or Rayne, until he could come across as calm and controlled even if he weren't feeling it. He picked up the silver-framed photo of Skye that sat on his desk. "You'll be the death of me, but damned if I won't die smiling." He replaced it with care before squaring his shoulders. An aura of confidence and control might have to be smoke and mirrors for a while.

When Luke got there, the staff dining room was full of laughter. The radio was playing in the kitchen next door and music threaded its way through the conversations. Tor was pouring mugs of tea from an enormous brown pot. Rayne and Skye were bickering over whether chocolate chip or oatmeal raisin were the best cookies.

"All my cookies are equally impressive," Tor said.

Rayne was the first to break into peals of laughter. "I'm sure your cookies are spectacular, chef." Rayne could barely contain himself.

"We're not talking about actual cookies anymore, are we?" Skye's eyes were wide, his cheeks stained pink.

Luke tried to align Skye's sweet naivety with recent events in his office. "Could we move the conversation away from Tor's cookies? I want my tea in a relaxed atmosphere with no discussion of Tor's, or anyone's, body parts involved. You seem to have become distracted from your task, Skye."

"I second that." Tor took a seat. "Even though recent events really deserve some attention." He didn't meet Luke's eyes.

"Sorry, Sir." Skye grabbed one of the mugs Tor had poured then handed it across to Luke.

"Cookies, people, I was talking about cookies!" Rayne's indignant expression was one hundred per cent fake. "You're all perverts."

"Lying equals spanking—we've discussed this before, brat." Tor gave Rayne a light cuff.

"You're not the boss of me." Rayne pouted.

"He is," Luke commented.

"I am." Tor gave a slow, lazy smile. "For the next two weeks at least."

"Well, damn." Rayne shoved a cookie in his mouth. "It's a conspiracy."

Luke was well aware that Rayne wasn't displeased with the situation. He wondered, as he had many times, how long it would take Rayne and Tor to get their act together and accept the feelings they had for each other. Skye had said they'd take their own sweet time, and he was probably right. Meanwhile they'd enjoy the no-strings arrangement that seemed to suit them for the time being. It was somewhat entertaining to watch Tor's slow smolder meet Rayne's thrust and parry.

"Tell us more about Zac, Sir. If you can," Skye said.

Luke sipped his tea, glad to have a topic that steered clear of clandestine blow jobs. Skye had redeemed himself a little. "It's not secret, but you know I haven't met him. I only have the information in his file and what I know from a few conversations with Mr. Hoffman."

"I think he must be very daring, traveling to a strange country on his own," Skye said.

"I think he's quite well traveled already, love. This won't be his first trip."

"Oh, I forgot…he's mega rich, isn't he?" Skye blushed. "I guess he's been all over the place."

"Well, his father is wealthy—that's not quite the same thing."

"It must be super hard to make friends without worrying whether people are only interested in his money. That makes me sad for him."

For the thousandth time Luke thought that Skye was the sweetest sub a man could wish for, with the biggest, softest heart. "A new friend for you then, and Rayne. He'll need other subs to talk to in between the Doms he's meeting."

"We'll look after him, won't we, Rayne?"

"Of course we will, if Tor ever lets me out of the kitchen." Rayne stuck his lower lip out even further.

"We won't be cooking for a house full, so you can stop pouting," Tor said. "You'll get the occasional five-minute break when I'm feeling generous."

Rayne blew a raspberry in Tor's direction, making Skye giggle.

"You two will need to be on your best behavior — setting a good example," Luke said, more for Rayne's benefit than Skye's.

Skye sat up straighter. "Of course! I hope he likes us." He nibbled on his lower lip.

"Of course he'll like us!" Rayne exclaimed. "What's not to love? He's friends with Alistair and Alistair loves us, so we're a natural extension. There's no need to worry, Skye."

"Don't forget when he arrives, he'll be jet lagged," Tor commented. "Don't talk his ear off when you collect him. You'll give the poor guy a headache before he even gets here."

"Hey!"

Luke held back a grin. Rayne had a way of expressing righteous indignation while still giving away his guilt. Rayne loved to talk, and they all knew it. Tor directed a glance at Rayne that told him he wasn't going to get away with anything. Rayne's expression said he'd try it anyway.

The easy exchanges and camaraderie between the men around the table gave Luke a warm glow inside. Tor, Rayne and of course Skye had become his family along with the other regular staff at The Retreat. Even Lucky and Marshmallow, the two cats they had adopted from a family left in a box by the gate, counted as part of their select little group.

We're a strange bunch, but somehow we work. Luke was looking forward to having Zac join them the following day. He loved when The Retreat's team was at its best, looking after whatever guests they had staying. A houseful was great, with the dungeon in regular use and the secrets of each of the color-themed bedrooms revealed to their excited occupants, but they had been fully booked for months and it would be nice to have the slight break that having a smaller number of people to look after meant.

Though he always made sure there was at least a day between each booking, that day was always filled with activity that it was hard to get done when they were all focused on the guests. Each of the staff had a day off a week in rotation, but Luke rarely took time for himself. He got antsy if he wasn't on hand to solve any problems that might come up. Tor had told him more than once that he was a control freak and he didn't bother denying it. His military background meant that he preferred everything to be planned in great detail. In his opinion, spontaneity was overrated.

"It's important we make a good impression both on Zac and on the Doms visiting him. Word of mouth is vital to our business here. It only takes one unhappy client to express dissatisfaction and word will get around, however unfair that might be. The community is small and news spreads. We want all these men to be waxing lyrical about how wonderful this place is."

"My food is enough to keep anyone happy," Tor declared. "The way to a man's heart is through his stomach — that's as true for subs and Doms as it is for anyone."

"We'll make everything perfect for them all," Skye said. "That's what we do." His confidence was endearing.

Luke let his gaze linger on the only man who could distract him from his job. Skye's violet eyes shone as he laughed and joked with Rayne. He had come out of his shell so much since arriving at The Retreat, but inside he was still the sweet, shy boy that Luke had fallen head over heels in love with. Love. A word that Luke would never have thought to apply to himself. Now its influence colored the way he did his job and he dearly hoped that all The Retreat's guests could experience the same happiness that he'd found with Skye.

Zac, however, was a bit of a conundrum, and Luke found that a bit unsettling. The arrangements they had made were highly unusual, but Carey had been careful in choosing the men that Zac would get to meet. They represented several different aspects of the BDSM lifestyle and, though the number of those aspects could be infinite, they would at least give Zac some limited experience of different tastes and styles. It would be intriguing to observe how everything went.

Luke drank his tea and contemplated the evening ahead. Time with Skye with no chance of interruption was something to be treasured. The shy glances that Skye kept sending his way told him that his sweet submissive was anticipating an enjoyable evening too.

Everything was right in Luke's world, and he was determined to relax and enjoy the moment. His mind drifted to all the wonderful, wicked things he would do to Skye that night to make him fly. For the next few hours, Skye would have his undivided attention, and he was determined that Skye's pleasure would come first for a while. *After a spanking, of course.*

Chapter Three

Zac took a deep breath, glad that the long journey from Arizona was finally over. He stretched, and several of his vertebrae clicked. "Jeez, that's penance for my mahoosive carbon footprint." He tilted his head to stare at the scudding clouds. "I'll plant a whole forest's worth of trees, okay?"

"Who are you talking to?" Rayne asked, coming to stand next to him.

"Whatever deity cares to listen and provide relief for my aching back."

"Not sure it works that way."

"Sadly, you're probably right. I'll get my bag from the boot." Zac hauled his suitcase from the boot of the car before his chauffeur could do it for him. He gave Rayne a sheepish grin. "Sorry, I'm determined to be self-sufficient on this trip." He rested the case on the gravel.

"Hey, I'm not gonna argue with guests who want to do my work for me," Rayne said, "I've never heard an

American use the term 'boot' before. I thought you guys were all about elephant appendages."

Zac snorted with laughter. "I'm Canadian. I've traveled all over the world. In my youth, we were in England for two years, and I got used to hearing it. I guess I learned it through osmosis, and it stuck." He grinned. "Would you prefer me to say things like 'yeehaw' and 'y'all'? Is that more in tune with American speak for you?"

Rayne slammed the boot shut, cackling. "I've never heard an American say 'yeehaw' either, except maybe in a Doris Day movie, and I've no idea what a Canadian would say. I thought you all spoke French." He shrugged. "I haven't traveled much at all—holidays with my folks involved a tent in a soggy field, a concrete shower block and a chemical toilet. Have you ever eaten tinned potatoes heated up over a Primus? I don't recommend it." He shuddered. "Now I've traumatized myself, let's change the subject. We made good time. I'm sure the welcoming committee is on the way."

Zac took a moment to take in his surroundings. The Retreat more than exceeded his expectations. Its atmospheric collection of Gothic architecture hung together better than it had any right to. He'd also been fascinated by the last part of the journey from the airport. The cool greens of the New Forest had been such a contrast from the browns of Arizona, and he'd even caught sight of sturdy ponies grazing between the trees. The woodland surrounding the property provided what felt like a cozy security blanket knitted from leaves and branches. The grounds had high walls and sturdy gates. He knew there were plenty of security precautions in place and the fact that he hadn't spotted them gave him confidence. The Retreat had a reputation for professionalism in every aspect of its operation, and Zac was grateful that his father had seen fit to allow him this opportunity.

And I'm going to make the most of it. After a nap. He yawned, jaw cracking. Rayne's expression was part amused, part sympathetic.

"First your back, now your jaw — you're falling apart."

"I swear I age a decade every time I fly. I need my feet on solid ground to recover."

"You must be exhausted. I've never flown long haul but I guess if I did my body wouldn't know which way was up for hours. I like my sleep."

"I napped on the plane," Zac said, "but I'm not a great flyer. It's claustrophobic and noisy. I know I shouldn't be complaining because not everyone gets the luxury of flying on a private jet. You must think I'm an over-privileged ingrate."

"I think your father cares about your security and I can imagine so many things I'd like to get up to on a private jet. The mile high club is still a thing, right? Did you have a hot air steward? And by have I mean…never mind, I'm going to get myself in trouble unless I zip my trap shut."

"I can see you're going to be a very bad influence on me, Rayne," Zac said. "I'm glad." He peered at dust rising in the distance. "I think we have company. I hope that isn't my first Dom arriving early. I really need to sleep if I'm going to make anywhere close to a half-decent impression."

A beaten-up yellow Mini hurtled down the last part of the drive into the courtyard, coming to a halt in a spray of gravel right in front of them.

"You think he's a rally driver?"

"Seems possible."

"I think the gravel's gonna need raking."

"Unfortunately, that's part of my job. I'm guessing he must be the new gardener," Rayne observed. "He's the only other person due to arrive today, and Luke would never have opened the gates if he wasn't a legitimate visitor. He really needs to park that crate around the back, though. He's lowering the tone."

"It has character," Zac said. "Have you ever seen the film *The Italian Job*, the one with the three Minis in it? It's one of my favorites. I don't think any of the cars in that were yellow, though." He looked on, curious, as the car's driver climbed out. He stretched and groaned, and Zac winced in sympathy just as The Retreat's front door swung open and a tall blond appeared on the step. From his military bearing, Zac guessed that he was Luke Redding, the general manager of The Retreat. Luke took in the scene, frowning.

"Rayne, stop dawdling. If you've unloaded all of Zak's luggage, you can go wash the car."

"Aw, you're no fun. I wanna meet the new guy." Rayne scuffed at the gravel, causing even more mess.

"If you aren't out of my sight in the next minute, young man, I'm going to send Tor round to the garages with instructions to turn your ass crimson."

"Yes, Sir, going, Sir."

"And make sure you rake the gravel later!"

Rayne ran for the car, giving Zac a quick wave as he went. "Good luck, Zac!"

Zac gulped and straightened his shoulders. Luke was the kind of man who commanded respect without asking for it. His steely gaze seemed to bore into Zac's soul.

"Zac, welcome to The Retreat. Please bear with me for one moment while I sort out the new gardener."

Zac nodded, trying to keep up. He was still assimilating the threat Luke had made to Rayne. If Zac wasn't mistaken, the general manager of The Retreat had just told one of his staff that he'd get a spanking if he didn't do as ordered. Zak's dick was apparently less jetlagged than the rest of him because it twitched with excitement. That was what *he* needed, craved even, a man prepared to take him in hand, a man who wasn't afraid to administer discipline when Zac got a little too cocky.

He turned his attention to the conversation going on between Mr. Redding and the man who appeared to be gardening's answer to the kind of model who appeared in advertising for leather gear. He was about the same height as Luke but more heavily built. He wore scuffed work boots, ripped jeans that hugged a pair of well-muscled thighs, and a plain black T-shirt. His exposed arms sported some interesting tattoos, and a long scar ran around one bicep. He was ruggedly good-looking, with hair shaved close to his scalp and three days' stubble but his most startling feature was his eyes, which were so dark they appeared close to black. He was the type of man that Zac dreamed about dropping to his knees in front of. He could only hope that the Doms he was going to meet over the next two weeks would be as attractive.

Though Zac would have been quite happy to stand and watch Luke and the hot gardener guy for the rest of the day, their conversation was short, and Luke soon returned to Zac's side.

"Sorry about that. With all the hours in the day, it was inevitable that the two of you would arrive at once." His tone was laced with sarcasm. "I guess you've probably had enough time to view our car parking area. Why don't we go inside? You must be desperate for a drink."

Zac appreciated Luke's efforts to put him at ease. "Sounds good. What I've seen so far is spectacular, even the parking lot."

"Is that a hint of brat I hear in your tone, Mr. Denman?"

"Not at all, Mr. Redding. I guess I got kind of dehydrated on the flight and it's affecting my ability to put together appropriate sentences."

Luke's expression was one of amused skepticism. "I can see you're going to give our visiting Doms a run for their money. I'll be sure to stock plenty of aloe in your bathroom." Zac didn't understand and it must have showed. Luke walked toward the huge oak front door. "It's a cooling gel, Zac. Perfect for soothing sore behinds."

Zac gaped. "Oh my God, either this is really happening, or I've fallen down the rabbit hole." He hefted his case and rushed after Luke only to come to a sudden halt in the front hall. "Wow, this place may not be The Savoy, but it really is something." A sweeping staircase led to a galleried landing and as Zac did a slow pirouette, he realized that the dappled, multi-colored light spilling through the hall came from a magnificent stained-glass window.

"Holy moly."

"The place makes a good first impression, doesn't it?" Pride shone in Luke's eyes.

"It sure does. So much better in real life than in the pictures I've seen."

"Ah yes, the secret website. You've met Carey Hoffman's partner, Alistair, haven't you? He took all the pictures for the site."

"I met Carey and Alistair at home in the States. My dad is a big fan of Alistair's work and so am I." Zac fought back another yawn. "He's incredibly talented."

"Usually, I'd get you settled then do the grand tour but I can see you're exhausted. I wouldn't recommend that you sleep for too long otherwise your body clock will never adjust, but perhaps a nap for an hour or two would be advisable."

"It would. I have to admit, I'm dying to see around the place but at the moment I don't think I could take everything in properly. I can hardly keep my eyes open. I'm sorry."

"Don't be. It's perfectly understandable. Let me take you to your room. There's a fridge in there if you need a drink or a light snack. You can get some rest, and I'll arrange for somebody to knock on your door in a couple of hours."

"Thank you, that sounds perfect." Zac followed Luke up the grand staircase, wondering which of the five doors would lead to the room he'd been allocated.

"Each of the rooms has its own secrets to discover," Luke said, "so what I decided to do was move you with each Dom so that you get to experience all of them over your stay. You'll be starting off in the green room. They're all color-themed in case you were wondering."

"If you're sure that's not too much work," Zac said, "it sounds like a great idea."

"We want you to have the best possible experience while you're here, Zac. Be assured that I and the rest of the staff will do everything in our power to make that happen. Nothing is too much trouble."

Luke opened the door to the green room, and Zac followed him inside. He immediately focused on the bed, which was made up in dark green and gold and looked supremely comfortable. He dropped his case on the floor and made a beeline for it, kicking off his shoes before throwing himself on to the well sprung mattress. He stretched out while Luke drew heavy curtains across the windows, shutting out the sunlight.

"Thanks, Luke, this bed is so comfortable." Zac's eyelids drooped.

"Rest well, Zac, you have some big adventures ahead of you."

"I'm sure I will." Zac was already halfway to sleep. He registered the soft click of the door closing as Luke left, then closed his eyes.

Luke headed downstairs to find Skye sitting on the bottom step, waiting for him.

"I was hoping to join you on the tour, Sir. Is Zac not feeling good?"

Luke held out a hand then pulled Skye to his feet. "He's fine, love. Just very tired after his long journey. He's taking a nap. You can wake him in an hour or two if you'd like to?"

"I would! I want to make friends and I know once his first Dom gets here, I won't have any time at all with him. He needs to know he has a friend he can talk to — another sub, you know?"

"And that has nothing to do with your curiosity."

Skye blushed. "Maybe a little. I do want him to feel welcome, though."

"I know you do. How about you come meet our new gardener instead? His name is Dale, and he arrived at the same time as Zac so I didn't have time to do more than send him around to the garages. I need to find him and apologize then give him a quick tour of the grounds."

"I'd love to." Skye bounced a little.

Luke chuckled. "Not so long ago you would have hidden in our room rather than meet someone new."

"But I'll be with you," Skye said, as if that explained everything. He slipped his hand into Luke's. "When I was new here, everyone was kind to me. It helped me settle in. Everyone who's new should know they're welcome, guests and gardeners."

"You have the softest heart." *And I'll do everything in my power to protect it.*

Skye leaned against him as they walked outside, circling the main building to the block which housed garaging for The Retreat's vehicles, under a small apartment used by Rayne. As they walked, Luke tried to work out in his head how he would talk to Dale. Skye was with him, and he didn't want Skye to know that Dale was more than a gardener.

Dale needed to operate beneath the radar in order to make the most of his role, and Skye's natural curiosity might lead him into places that Dale didn't need him to be. Luke also didn't want Skye sharing information with Zac and if the two of them became friends, which Luke could easily see happening, Skye wouldn't be able to keep secrets. It was impossible for him to dissemble — his innate honesty meant that everything was revealed on his face. Any attempt to lie, and he went crimson.

Dale was leaning against the bonnet of his Mini, dark glasses shading his eyes, his head tilted back as if he were soaking up the sun. On the surface, he seemed relaxed, but as a military man Luke recognized the signs that said he was ready for action. There was a slight tension about Dale, and he was very still. Luke guessed that had he been able to see Dale's eyes, he would be scanning his surroundings, taking in every small detail. He didn't think the man was ever anything but alert.

The battered car seemed incongruous next to the other sleek, well-kept vehicles in The Retreat's immaculate garages.

"She's the poor relative, isn't she?" Dale strolled toward Luke with a smile. "But she gets me from A to B and doesn't complain about being filled with tools or bags of compost."

"I had one in my late teens, so cheap it was more rust than car, held together by gaffer tape and sheer bloody mindedness. I'm sorry I wasn't able to spend more time with you earlier, Dale. We have one guest for the next couple of weeks, and you both managed to arrive at the same time."

Dale removed his sunglasses, revealing his piercing eyes. "Nice to meet you, Mr. Redding, and no problem. Guests come first—if Carey heard otherwise he'd rescind my dungeon privileges at The Underground."

"That he would. This is my partner and submissive, Skye. You'll be seeing him around the place while you're here, and I'll introduce you to Tor, our chef, and Rayne, who's usually our driver but will be helping out in the kitchen for a while. Other than that, we have the one guest I mentioned—his name is Zac—and several visitors due over the next two weeks."

"I doubt they'll be seeing much of me," Dale said, "I'm good at keeping out of the way."

"Well, this is where you'll be staying." Luke gestured to the apartment above the garages. "Rayne normally lives here but he's moved into the main house because he needs to be close to the kitchen while he's assisting the chef out. I hope you'll be comfortable here."

"I'm sure I will be." Dale took the key that Luke handed over. "All I need's a bed, bathroom and a kettle. Everything else I can make up as I go along."

"You'll find the tool shed in the grounds, it's pretty obvious and the combination to the padlock is six-nine-six-nine, someone's idea of humor. If there's anything you need, you have my number or come find me in my office. Skye will always get a message to me as well."

"I will." Skye bounced a little. "I like to walk in the grounds and I'm easy to spot." He tugged at a lock of silver hair.

"Thank you, Skye, I'll keep a look out for you."

Luke was pleased at the gentle smile Dale bestowed on Skye. "Dale is going to be working on extending Tor's herb garden and installing some new raised beds so that we can grow more of our own organic vegetables, Skye."

"Oh wow! That means Tor's cooking will taste even better, and I didn't think that was possible. He's an amazing chef, Dale. I hope you'll be able to join us for staff meals."

"I hope so too, Skye. Mr. Redding, if you have them, I'd appreciate some plans of the house and grounds. I need to know the layout for positioning."

"Of course. I'll send them to your email, and call me Luke."

"Perfect. I have my laptop with me so I'll scout out the grounds today then start work in the morning."

"Would you like me to show you around?"

"I'd prefer to explore on my own, if that's okay with you?"

"Of course. We'll leave you to get sorted," Luke said. "Otherwise Skye will be asking you a never ending stream of questions about composting."

"Sir, it's good stuff! Oh, you need to tell Dale about Lucky and Marshmallow."

Dale gave Luke a quizzical look.

"Cats," Luke explained. "Mother and daughter. They have their beds and food in the back of the garage, which means you'll likely see them around. They are effective mousers and keep rabbits out of the vegetables, so they earn their keep. I should have asked if you were allergic."

"I love cats *and* dogs for that matter. Do you need me to feed them?"

"No, Skye or Rayne will deal with them, please don't worry. They'll probably try to sneak into the flat. Rayne lets them roam but they aren't supposed to come into the main building."

"But sometimes they do," Skye added, guilt written large across his face.

"And we all know why that is," Luke said, exasperated.

"They're so cute," Skye defended.

"And I let you, and by default them, walk all over me. I need to be stricter."

Dale chuckled. "I'm happy to offer hard labor as an option. A few hours clearing brambles can do wonders for a sub's attitude."

Skye's eyes widened.

"I'll keep that in mind for the next time I catch a feline curled up in my office chair," Luke said.

"Sir, you wouldn't! Brambles are mean and scratchy!"

"And Marshmallow sheds more fur than a fully grown golden retriever. Do you have any idea how much I spend on lint roller refills?"

Dale guffawed. "Cats do have a way of making their presence felt."

"You love them too, Sir, I know you do. You talk to them when you think I'm not listening." Skye's lips were set in a determined line, and Luke knew when to beat a hasty retreat.

"Now, our new guest is napping, but I have a few things to do before I let Skye wake him. You know where I am if you need me, Dale. We'll see you for dinner at seven, just follow your nose."

"I will." Dale hefted his duffel and turned toward the carriage house.

Luke took Skye's hand as they returned to the main building. "He seems nice, Sir," Skye said. "He's a Dom, isn't he?"

"You caught the vibe, did you?"

"Well I know that most of the people who work here are into the lifestyle to some extent but I don't like to make assumptions. Some of our fiercest, scariest guests have turned out to be the subbiest subs ever."

"They have, and you're right not to judge, but in this case you're on the mark. Dale is a Dom and ex-military like me, though not the same branch of the services. He's ex-army like Tor and he's a member at The Underground — a friend of Carey's."

"You won't mind if I talk to him a little bit about composting, will you? I promise not to disturb him if he's working."

"As long as Dale doesn't mind, it's fine with me."

"I'll bet he keeps the vegetables in order. No weed will dare make an appearance."

"I'm not sure plants respond to dominance in quite the same way as subs, love."

Skye pouted. "They so do. It's all about the atmosphere. My cactus likes me to talk to her and she likes music too."

"I stand corrected." Luke was not about to head down that particular rabbit hole. He gave Skye's hand a squeeze. "How about you and I go check that everything's in order in the dungeon? We have an hour before you need to wake Zac."

"Oh! Yes please, Sir." Skye moved a bit faster. "I really want to see the new spanking bench that was delivered yesterday."

"It would be wise to give it a test drive," Luke said, admiring the light pink flush that spread from Skye's throat to his face.

"Wouldn't want it collapsing at an inopportune moment, Sir. It's the responsible thing to do."

"Quite." Luke couldn't wait to see Skye's bare skin against deep red leather, his limbs strapped in place, ass exposed. *A little self-indulgent, but what the heck. We both need an occasional treat.*

Chapter Four

Dale dropped his duffel on the bed, which was covered in a dark green tartan blanket. He had a look around what would be his home for the next two weeks. The apartment above the garages was long and thin but had plenty of light from a combination of windows and skylights. The bedroom was at one end, bathroom at the other with a kitchen-diner-lounge combo in the middle. It seemed to have been given a fresh coat of cream paint and was spotless. It was compact but had everything he could possibly need for his stay. *Very nice. I've bunked down in a lot worse places, that's for sure.*

He sat on the bed while he unpacked his bag, unloading his laptop, a dog-eared paperback and washbag. The clothes he left where they were. He needed to get his tech set up first, link to The Retreat's security system, get oriented about the layout of the place. His mind, however, kept straying to the brief glimpse he'd caught of the man he was going to be protecting. He shook his head. Zac Denman was off-limits. He was young, rich, and could have his pick of men. Carey had no doubt set him up with the best of the best when it came to available Dominants while Dale would be spending his nights lurking in the undergrowth. He gave a low chuckle. At least he was accustomed to disappearing into the background. He'd be watching boundaries and security feeds, not enticing green eyes and glossy dark hair.

A little stiff after his drive, Dale decided to delay setting up in favor of a stroll around the grounds while it was still light. The evenings were starting to draw in, and he didn't want his first survey to be done in the dark. He needed to stretch his legs and take in some fresh air.

What he'd seen of The Retreat so far had impressed him. He'd heard about it of course, the place was the stuff of legends amongst the membership at The Underground, and the idea of one day bringing his own sub for a break had appeal. He admired and had a lot of respect for Carey Hoffman, so when Carey had asked a favor, Dale didn't even have to think about it. He loved his landscaping and garden design business but every now and again it felt good to revive some of his more…specialist skills.

He navigated the steps then paused to admire the vehicles stored in the open-fronted garages. One vintage Morgan in particular caught his eye. A pang of guilt struck him as he passed his Mini, tucked in a corner, and he gave her an apologetic glance.

As he walked, a few twinges in his hip reminded him about the reason for his career change. He gave a wry smile. He wouldn't recommend getting shot to anyone…it definitely wasn't like in the movies where the hero seemed to be able to take a bullet then carry on after the application of a bandage and perhaps a swig of brandy. Reality was a whole different mess of pain, blood, infection and agonizing recuperation. Dale had been lucky not to lose his leg or his ability to walk. He *had* lost the career he loved and excelled at but was a firm believer in the mantra what doesn't kill you makes you stronger — even if the 'stronger' part was bullshit if applied to physical rather than psychological health. He gave a mental shrug. He'd long come to terms with what had happened. He'd known the risks when he'd signed up, and the armed forces had given him some very good years and a lot of solid friends, some of whom hadn't made it home at all. That had put everything into perspective during long hours of torture masquerading as physical therapy. He put the past out of his head to concentrate on the present and the job in hand.

Above the walls that surrounded the grounds of The Retreat, a dense curtain of trees rustled and waved in the breeze. The unique scent of the forest sparked memories of a childhood trip, camping with his parents and younger sister for one magical week in the school holidays when he was ten or eleven. Dale recalled picnics by the river, sultry evenings in pub beer gardens with warm bottled Coke and spying ponies through the trees. They'd been blessed with a rare week of fine weather, not dissimilar to the current conditions — a rarity because his other holiday memories were rain-soaked, windswept and tended to involve umbrellas and windbreaks. Even though the forest was beautiful in fine weather, he'd have preferred storms and rain because criminals liked decent weather as much as the next man. Downpours would also keep Zac tucked up safe inside The Retreat.

The grounds were a mix of manicured landscaping and areas that had been left wilder. A rough path ran around the boundary, which Dale followed for a while. The high wall was embedded on the top with shards of glass, but that wouldn't be much of a deterrent for a determined interloper. In some places huge oaks grew close to the walls, their limbs crossing the boundary, providing another possible means of ingress. Dale noted the locations of carefully positioned security cameras, which wouldn't have been easy to spot by anyone other than an expert. Carey Hoffman had invested in state-of-the-art systems installed by professionals and that eased Dale's mind a little, but the place wasn't Fort Knox. There was also more acreage than he'd be able to keep a constant eye on even with the help of the cameras.

Mulling a few options over in his mind, he retraced his steps until he reached the gate to the kitchen garden and was impressed to find a pattern of beds bristling with vegetables, fruit bushes, and herbs. "Very nice," he murmured.

"Do my veg beds have an admirer?" Belatedly, Dale spotted the man who spoke, concealed behind a bamboo cane pyramid bearing the weight of prolific runner bean plants. "I'm Tor Halvorsen, the chef."

"The outfit's a bit of a giveaway," Dale said.

Tor was wearing checked trousers and a spotless white jacket. The only thing missing was a tall white hat. He gave Dale a disarming grin. "You must be the new gardener."

Dale nodded as he shook Tor's hand. "That would be me. The name's Dale. I'm just exploring a bit—needed to ease out a few kinks after the drive down."

"You'll find plenty of kinks around here," Tor said, straight-faced.

"So I've heard. This place is the stuff of legend at The Underground."

"Everything you've heard is true...especially if it's about my cooking."

"Something I can't wait to test for myself. This is a spectacular kitchen garden. If this is the result of your efforts, you have remarkable green fingers as well as culinary skills. I'm looking forward to working on the expansion for you."

"I wish I could take the credit, but there's a small team that usually looks after the grounds and gardens here. I only make use of the results."

"Well, I could burn water so I covet home cooking wherever I can get it. I guess Mr. Redding has told you he's invited me to eat with the staff."

"He has, and you're very welcome. I'm used to cooking for a lot more than the handful of folk here for the next two weeks so I hope you've got a good appetite."

"You put it in front of me, and I'll eat it."

"You're giving away your army past," Tor said, grinning.

"I guess that means you're ex-services too?"

"Also army. Luke, Mr. Redding, was in the navy but he's not all bad."

"Nobody's perfect. Someone had to drive the boats to get us where we needed to be, right? Perhaps we can share some tall tales over dinner tonight. Who else is going to be there?"

"Well you've already met Luke and joking aside, he's a great guy. You're in the lifestyle, right?"

Dale nodded. "I don't think I'd be here if I wasn't, do you?"

"He's a great Dom, too. Did you meet his sub, Skye?"

"I did. That boy is exceptionally pretty."

"That he is. Sweet as well, unlike Rayne the chauffeur, who will also be joining us tonight."

"Red hair, cheeky?"

"That's him."

"I caught a glimpse of him when I arrived earlier. He'd just got back with a guest. Zac I think Luke said his name was."

"Picked him up from the airport. He came in from the States on a private jet and has a few Doms set up to test him out, I believe. More than that I can't say."

"This place has a well-deserved reputation for discretion. I don't need to know about him, I doubt he'll be touring the vegetable garden any time soon."

"I'm not expecting him in the kitchen either. Not yet, anyway."

"Sounds intriguing."

"According to Luke, one of the Doms coming over the next two weeks is into domestic discipline, so you never know. He might want our trainee sub washing dishes naked."

Dale chuckled. "That would be entertaining. And you and Rayne? Forgive me if I'm way off base here, but I get the sense that there's something…"

"Let's just say that my spanking hand has a close relationship with that boy's ass. Trouble is, he enjoys it way too much." Tor rolled his eyes. "We are getting to know each other… Not sure I'm ready for my own sub at the moment but Rayne loves to play, and we are pretty isolated here. We don't get the opportunity to go up to London that often so I'm lucky that Rayne is willing to indulge me."

"My visits to The Underground can be a bit sporadic. I go where the work is, which means central London is often out of reach. Don't get me wrong, I enjoy seeing different places, but it would be great to be able to play more often. I've never had a bad night there, and it's a great place to hang out with like-minded people if I just fancy company and conversation. This is a spectacular area. Haven't been here since I was a kid."

"It's unique. I can't imagine calling anywhere else home. I hope this spell of good weather holds for you, it can't be much fun digging in a quagmire. My garden is yours… I'm not going to interfere but the more space you can prep for us the better. We get through a vast amount of produce. I'm afraid I need to get on. Dinner won't cook itself. Rayne is supposed to be helping me and is going to take some wrangling."

"Good luck with that. I'm going to check out the toolshed. The glamour never ends."

Laughing, his arms laden with vegetables and herbs, Tor headed back toward the house. Dale watched him go, noting the door he used to gain access. It was a shame that he'd had to be less than honest with Tor because he felt he could be a useful ally. He resolved to have a word with Luke about bringing Tor into their small circle of confidence.

After spending the next couple of hours familiarizing himself with the contents of the toolshed, the grounds and the layout of the buildings that made up The Retreat, Dale made his way back to the garages, intending to take a nap before the evening meal. He had to sleep when he could, knowing that as well as keeping up a front as a gardener he would be spending a lot of the night hours on alert.

As he passed the back of the house, a flicker of movement caught his eye. He glanced up to see that someone was drawing back the drapes in one of the first-floor rooms. Partly concealed by a row of rhododendrons, Dale paused to watch when he realized that the room's occupant was Zac. He was shirtless, his body trim. He stretched, yawned, then opened the window. Leaning forward, he took a deep breath and a smile spread across his face. Dale smiled with him, wishing he could see more below the level of the windowsill.

Wonder if he's naked in there. Wow, since when did voyeurism become my thing? He shook his head and moved away, careful to stay hidden. He could justify his interest in Zac because he was being paid to keep an eye on him, but he still felt sleazy. He needed to remain professional, not get distracted by ogling the beautiful boy.

In the remaining time before dinner, Dale set all his security feeds up to his satisfaction, took a nap then a shower and made a few calls to check up on his business. By the time he needed to make his way to the staff dining room, his stomach was rumbling. He'd have to ask Tor for some snacks. He was addicted to wine gums and had exhausted his supply on the drive down. *If he's even a half-decent chef, he should have a supply. No pantry should be without wine gums.*

Dale did as Luke had suggested and followed his nose to the kitchen. The most amazing smells were issuing from the doorway as he approached. Luke and Skye were already seated at a table in the room next to the kitchen.

"Dale, I hope you've settled in," Luke said. "Welcome to the staff dining room."

"I have, thank you. I got my bearings, checked out the grounds then took a nap and freshened up a bit. I must thank Rayne for the loan of his apartment. The bed is exceptionally comfortable. It's a good job I set an alarm or I might have missed dinner altogether."

"That would have been a tragedy," Skye said, looking anxious. "Tor's cooking is not to be missed."

"So my nose is telling me. I met Tor earlier in the garden."

"He'll be here shortly," said Luke. "I imagine he'll be making Rayne earn his keep by serving us."

No sooner had Luke spoken than Tor came through from what Dale assumed to be the kitchen and joined them at the table. His face was a little flushed and his hair disheveled. He sank into a chair.

"I swear, that boy will be the death of me. He needs to be taught how to follow instructions. He seems to think obedience is optional. I had to restart the sauce twice because of him distracting me." He grabbed a glass of water and took a long drink.

Dale was amused by the vibe around the table. Skye was trying desperately not to laugh, and even Luke was having trouble keeping a straight face. Dale guessed that the ongoing relationship between Tor and Rayne was a source of constant entertainment at The Retreat.

"You need to use a firm hand with him," Luke said.

Tor scowled. "My palm aches from the number of spankings I've given that brat. He needs a nice heavy collar, leash and a cock cage."

"I'm sure he'd be more than happy for you to deliver all three."

"If I had his dick locked up and possession of the key, he might be a bit more respectful. What must you think of us, Dale? A so-called BDSM retreat, and we can't even control our own staff," Tor grumbled.

The need to respond was circumvented by Rayne coming in from the kitchen with a laden tray. He deposited three steaming dishes on the table then returned to the kitchen, an exaggerated sway to his hips. Dale kept an eye on Tor as Rayne made several trips before everything was finally on the table. Tor had narrowed his eyes, and Dale thought he could detect a slight twitch below one of them. Rayne didn't utter a word but made sure to brush against Tor's side several times before taking the seat next to him and sitting demurely with his hands folded in his lap. Dale wasn't convinced by the act. He could spot a mischievous sub a mile away, and Rayne was clearly a prize brat.

"Help yourselves, everyone," Luke said. "It would be a crime for this wonderful meal to go cold. What was your contribution, Rayne?"

"I got to peel potatoes, chop vegetables and do the washing up," Rayne said, pouting. "Tor wouldn't let me do anything important."

Tor sighed. "All jobs in the kitchen are important and besides, I had to teach you how to peel a potato," he said, sounding disgusted as he helped himself to a big scoop of creamy mash. "And show you how to use a bean slicer." There were also dishes of baked salmon, home-made parsley sauce and runner beans.

"The beans, herbs and potatoes are all from the garden," Tor said. "I'm afraid we don't run to our own salmon farm quite yet."

"It all looks amazing," Dale said. "I travel with work so much that it's rare I get a decent home-cooked meal…if I'm not mistaken I think there's someone here who may like to join us." They all swiveled toward the door, and Zac edged inside.

"I'm so sorry to interrupt your meal. I hope you don't mind. Mr. Redding, you said I could have a tray in my room but it's a little lonely and I wondered if…well, Skye suggested I might like some company. If I'm imposing, do say so."

"You're very welcome, Zac," Luke said.

"Sit." Dale patted the empty chair next to him.

Zac, it seemed, did not have a problem with obedience. He sat wide-eyed, lips slightly parted. Dale put a plate together for him, and Zac gave him a grateful smile.

"Thank you, Sir." He snapped his mouth shut.

"Dale will do for now." *Though Sir or Master would be preferable.* Dale decided that eating was a good plan as several sets of eyes were resting on him. After a second's awkward delay everyone else began tucking in too with various exclamations of delight at the wonderful meal.

"I always cook extra," Tor said. "You can join us any time, Zac."

"I appreciate it. I guess I'm a little anxious. Being on my own gives me too much time to think about what's going to happen over the next two weeks."

Dale wanted nothing more than to put his arm around Zac's shoulders and lend him some comfort. *It's not my place. I've already overstepped.* He spotted Luke give Skye a nudge.

"You don't need to worry, you know." Skye was so quietly spoken that everyone stopped clattering their cutlery to listen to him. "You'll be in control. Nothing happens that you don't want in a D/s relationship, even a play session. The sub holds all the power. That's right, isn't it, Sir?"

"Yes it is, sweetheart. Very well put."

Dale found himself nodding, as did Tor.

"Any good Dom will always respect your safe word. They'll check you're into the scene. Mr. Hoffman would never send anyone to play with you who he didn't trust, so you can relax," Tor said.

"If you decide you only want to share milk and cookies with them," Rayne said, "that's what'll happen." He nodded as if confirming his own statement. Tor looked heavenward.

"I don't think I just want that," Zac whispered.

"Oh, if you want all the kinky stuff, that's good too. Very good. Very, very good." Rayne helped himself to more mashed potatoes.

Dale focused on his food. He found he didn't much like the idea of Zac enjoying 'kinky stuff' with anyone else. He fancied Zac was leaning a fraction closer to him. *You're imagining things, idiot. You're the help as far as he's concerned.*

"Much as I hate to admit it, Zac, Rayne's right. Though Skye put it better," Tor said. "If everyone's had enough, you can take the empty dishes to the kitchen, brat, then bring in dessert."

"Never let anyone tell you that kitchens are not dictatorships," Rayne muttered. "Chefs are worse than Mussolini, Pol Pot and that North Korean dude all rolled into one." He cast a baleful glare in Tor's direction before stalking to the kitchen, balancing a pile of dishes.

Tor shrugged. "He's not wrong. There's no room in a good kitchen for more than one boss."

"And you love ordering him around," Luke stated.

Tor quirked his lips into a half-smile, giving himself away. Dale snuck a look at Zac to find him laughing, his eyes bright. He seemed relaxed and happy. The banter amongst this found family had achieved exactly the right result.

"Wow," Dale exclaimed, as Rayne returned carting an enormous cut glass dish of trifle. "I haven't had proper trifle since I spent Christmas at my nan's about fifteen years ago."

"I added the sherry," Rayne proclaimed.

"Don't worry, I was supervising," Tor clarified. "We won't all need hangover cures in the morning."

"Good to know. Gardening with a pounding headache isn't fun." Dale had been there once after a mate's twenty-fifth birthday party where grain and grape had been liberally mixed. It hadn't been pretty.

Rayne took charge of ladling out sizeable helpings.

"I don't think I've ever had this," Zac said as he spooned some into his mouth. "It's good, though. I'm going to have to take advantage of the gym and the pool here if you keep feeding me like this."

"At your age, you probably burn calories by breathing," Tor said. "And if that came across as jealousy, that's exactly what it was."

Luke grunted his agreement. "And that's why I run around the perimeter every morning. You'd be welcome to join me while you're here, Dale."

"Sounds good." *And it'll provide an opportunity to keep Luke up to date with any security concerns, which is probably why he's mentioned it.*

"You're welcome to use the pool too, outside working hours."

"That would be great. I've an old hip injury and it plays up sometimes. I can't always run, but swimming is a bit kinder on the body."

"How did you get hurt, if you don't mind me asking?" Zac asked, forehead creased in concern.

"I was slow. Failed to get out of the way of a bullet."

Zac's eyes widened, and Skye gasped. Rayne leaned forward, elbows on the table and gestured with his spoon. "Tell us, Dale!"

"Dale might not be comfortable sharing that part of his past," Luke cautioned.

Dale shrugged. "It's ancient history. Let's just say I won't be going back to Afghanistan any time soon."

"How about you, Tor and I have a coffee in the banqueting hall," Luke suggested. "Skye lit the fire in there earlier so it will be nice and warm. We can exchange military stories, and you two can try to convince me that the army is superior to the navy, which it isn't." There was a definite note of challenge in Luke's voice.

"Rayne and Skye can load the dishwasher," Tor said.

"And me," Zac offered. "I can help. I'd love to spend some time with you guys, if you don't mind?"

"Of course we don't," Skye said, smiling. "We can form our own subs' club, it'll be fun."

Tor and Luke exchanged worried glances, and Dale held back a laugh.

Muttering something about impending doom, Tor went to the kitchen to make coffee. Dale leaned back in his seat, content to observe for a while, and if his gaze settled more often than not on Zac, he didn't think anyone noticed.

Chapter Five

The following morning, Dale ran with Luke. His hip ached a little, but it was nothing he couldn't cope with, and it felt good to stretch his legs. It was a fresh, cool day, the dew thick on the grass and there was a light mist which swirled around their feet in places. Luke set a good pace but seemed pleased to have company. Dale kept up with him easily enough, though he suspected Luke may have been holding back. When they finished their circuit of the grounds they stopped to stretch outside the garages.

"Same time tomorrow?" Luke wasn't even breathing heavily.

Dale nodded. "If you don't mind keeping it slow for me."

"Just breaking you in gently. It's much nicer having someone to run with."

"It's also a great way of doing a check the perimeter without being too obvious. Doesn't Tor run?"

"He prefers the rowing machine in the gym and he uses the free weights. That's not my thing. I like being outdoors because I spend most of the day inside. Tor is in and out to the gardens."

"Being outside is the best thing about my job—I don't enjoy being cooped up either."

"What are you going to do today?" Luke asked.

"Start establishing my persona as an innocent gardener by laying out Tor's raised beds. I intend to knock off early and get a few hours' sleep so that I can be awake overnight. I don't think Zac is at risk during the day so long as he doesn't wander off."

"Do you think he's at risk at all?"

"If I were of a criminal inclination, I'd see his presence here as an opportunity. Not because it's not secure but because it's different for him. He won't be on the alert like he must be at home. He's going to be focused on the reason for his trip, distracted by the excitement of it all. He's young, testing his submission for the first time, I doubt he'll give more than a passing thought to anything else and I don't blame him. If, and it's a big if, anyone has tracked him here I'd expect them to attempt to get a look inside the grounds. After dark I'm going to fit a few remote cameras on the approach roads. They're battery powered so they won't last too long, but they don't need to. Cameras can be a defense strategy too. Professionals might spot them. They won't disable them because that would be a giveaway. They'll be forced into narrower means of access."

"And that makes your job a bit simpler."

"I'm glad you didn't say easier. You have a very long boundary here so closing down options is important. While I think of it, I was going to suggest that you share why I'm here with Tor. He's observant. He's going to wonder why I'm not making enough progress in the garden and he'll be a useful ally. With you, me and Tor alert to anything suspicious alongside all the security precautions, we'll be in a good place."

"Okay, I don't have a problem with bringing him into the fold. I probably should have included him from the start, but Carey asked me to limit the number of people who knew about you. What about Rayne and Skye?"

"They'll be spending too much time with Zac, and I don't want any of them upset or worrying. It's not fair."

"I agree. Though it's likely Skye will give me hell for not telling him when he eventually finds out. He's as protective of me as I am of him."

"Good subs want to take care of their Doms."

"You sound a little wistful, if you don't mind me saying?"

"Maybe." Dale stood with his hands on his hips. "I see established couples like you and Skye, like Alistair and Carey and others at The Underground, and I think it may be time for me to find someone of my own."

"Someone like Zac, perhaps?"

Dale rubbed a hand over his head. "What makes you say that?"

"I'm observant. I've noticed you watching him and I don't think it's because you're here to protect him."

"I won't deny I find him appealing but he's way out of my league. I'm here to do a job. I can't be distracted by pipe dreams." Luke didn't respond, and Dale considered the subject closed. "Tomorrow morning then?"

"Sure, I'll look forward to it. Have a good day. You know where to find me if you need anything. Zac's first

Dom is due to arrive tomorrow morning. I'll email you a picture and details of his car as you may not have met him. He and all the other Doms have been vetted at The Underground, and Carey trusts them implicitly. There's no way he'd send anyone near Zac if he had even the slightest concern."

Dale nodded. "I'm sure. If we have to worry about anyone, they'll likely be from further afield."

Luke returned to the main building and Dale went back to his temporary home to take a shower and change into work gear. For a while at least he needed to be a gardener.

Once he'd gotten clean and dressed, he grabbed a bowl of cereal from the supplies left for him, not wanting to bother Tor. He ate watching the breakfast news feeling detached from the outside world within the confines of The Retreat. He made a quick call to Carey to let him know he'd arrived and passed on a few first impressions of the security situation.

"Luke is on top of everything, but he's not blind to the issues of the boundary. The Retreat's seclusion has its advantages but there are downsides too." He explained his plan to become more nocturnal while keeping up his cover. "Luke doesn't want to worry Skye, Rayne or Zac. I have asked him to brief Tor on the real reason for my presence because I could use the extra set of eyes."

"I'm leaving this in your hands, Dale," Carey said. "Don't work yourself to the point of exhaustion, though. There's a limit to what you can do, and you have excellent technology to help you."

"I won't but I'd hate for anything to happen to Zac. He's a nice kid."

"Hardly a kid. He's twenty-two."

Dale grunted. "Young and therefore not afraid of anything."

"Do I detect an interest beyond protecting him?" Carey's knowing tone made Dale wince.

"Not you too. I had Luke questioning my motives earlier. I'm here to do a job, that's it."

"Have you spent any time with Zac?"

"He joined the staff for dinner yesterday evening. Helped to wash up and everything."

"He doesn't fit the stereotype of a spoiled rich kid, does he? He's had a solid upbringing. I've met his father and I liked him a lot."

"Even so. He lives in a completely different sphere to me."

"Possibly. I think his sphere is a mystery to most of us. However, over the next two weeks he's one of us, and I want his introduction to our world to be as smooth and painless as possible. Well, not necessarily painless but you know what I mean."

Dale chuckled. "On that note, Carey, I think I'll be getting to work. I have vegetable beds to build."

"And a fine vocation that is when the resulting produce ends up in Tor's kitchen."

"Go eat breakfast, Carey. I think your stomach's doing the talking."

"You are correct, and I can smell bacon. So goodbye." Carey rang off before Dale could say anything else.

"I guess nothing comes between that man and his bacon." Dale gave his cereal bowl and mug a rinse then left them on the draining board. He donned his boots at the door then took the stairs to ground level. What he noticed most, as he walked across the grounds to the kitchen garden, was the quiet. Apart from the continual rustle of leaves and various bird calls, there was no other sound. No traffic, no construction, no voices. Dale took a deep breath, sucking in the clean air then letting it out, his shoulders relaxing as he did. He was quite happy to exchange the sounds of the city with those of the forest for a while.

As he approached his destination, Dale was surprised to see a figure in the distance. He wasn't expecting anyone to be there but if Luke had discussed the real reason for his presence with Tor, he guessed the chef might want a quick word. Drawing closer, he realized that it wasn't Tor who was waiting, but Zac, who was sitting on a low wall near the house, face turned to the sun. He had on a pair of ripped jeans and a Nirvana tour T-shirt that had to have belonged to his father.

"Where did you get those boots?" Tor asked, coming to a stop in front of Zac.

"Jesus! You sure move quietly for a big guy." Zac got to his feet. "I take the same size as Rayne. He lent them to me."

"And why are you here?"

"I have a whole other day to wait until my first Dom arrives and to say I'm a bit fidgety would be an understatement. Luke suggested that you might appreciate a laborer for the day, so here I am. I should warn you, though, apart from the spider plant I had at college, I don't have much experience with keeping green things alive. I'd love to have had a room full of plants but there was never enough time and I'd have had to keep moving them around. Trevor was undemanding."

"Trevor?"

"My spider plant." Zac gave Dale a sheepish smile.

"Good to know, but we won't be planting anything for a while. This really will be hard labor. Clearing, digging, shifting barrow loads of compost, building the wooden frames... If you're still up for it, you're welcome to join me."

"I'm all yours." Zac's cheeky grin sent a stab of lust to Dale's groin. "For today at least."

"You do what I say, when I say it. Understand?"

"If I didn't already know, I'd definitely peg you as a Dom," Zac said. "You like to be in charge, don't you?"

Dale scowled. "I do. Deal with it." Dale wasn't sure he could handle an entire day working with Zac without doing something unprofessional, but his desire to spend time with the intriguing young man outweighed his common sense. "Show me your hands." Zac jumped down from his perch on the wall then held his hands out for inspection. "The first thing we're going to have to do is find you some gloves."

"You can tell I've not done much manual labor, then?"

Dale shook his head. "You've been at university, haven't you? I guess there's not much call for handling tools and digging unless you were studying archaeology and I don't want you damaging your hands."

"Biology, actually, with a minor in Latin."

"Interesting choices. What do you intend to do as a career?"

"Well, it sounds kind of weird, but I'd really like to work for a seed depository sourcing samples for the collections and propagating rare plants. I know it's not as sexy or appealing as something involving animal conservation or even marine biology, but plants are amazing. Trevor survived, I'm up for more difficult botanical challenges."

"Have you ever been to Kew?" Dale began walking across to the toolshed where he was sure he'd seen several sets of work gloves.

"No, but I'd love to go there. I have some time after my stay here before I have to go back to the States so I'm hoping to take it in and maybe visit some botanical gardens. I'd also like to get down to the Eden project in Cornwall but I guess it will depend on whether Dad can find somebody to provide security for that kind of trip and if he doesn't want me with him. He usually goes to the Far East at this time of year, and I often go along to act as his assistant." He looked downcast, and Dale wanted to draw him into a comforting hug. He settled for what he hoped was an empathetic smile.

"I can't imagine what it's like, but it must be tough, having to worry about security all the time."

"I'm kinda used to it. I was the target of more than one kidnapping attempt as a kid and thanks to my father's precautions, none of them succeeded. The last thing I need is to cause him aggravation by getting picked up by a bunch of criminals. It's inconvenient, but the alternative isn't great. Being here is a huge relief because it gives me a chance to relax for a while without having to worry about that stuff. Luke seems really confident. Kind of intimidating, actually. Skye is a very lucky man."

"Is Luke your type then?"

"No, I just mean that Skye is incredibly fortunate to have found a Dom who understands him and knows exactly what he needs. He's so calm when they're together. He always looks like he thinks Luke hung the moon and when Luke is with Skye, their love is clear as crystal. Who wouldn't be a bit envious of that? As for my type, I prefer my men to be a little rougher around the edges." He shook his head. "My men. If only. I make it sound like I know what I'm talking about."

Dale didn't think the slight pink tinge on Zac's cheeks was a result of the cool breeze. Dale wondered if his face was betraying him too.

"Staying here is a good way to change that."

"You know all about why I'm here then?"

"I don't know the details, only what came up over dinner last night."

"I don't mind you knowing. You're a Dom too."

A frustrated one at this moment. They reached the shed where Dale put the combination into the padlock then opened the door. It was a lot bigger than the average garden store, more like a garage in fact, as there was a ride-on mower parked inside. There still wasn't that much room to maneuver, however, and Dale found himself very close to Zac. Along one wall sat an ancient workbench with shelves beneath. It was well ordered and apart from some stray bits of grass and the odd cobweb, very clean.

"Mr. Redding doesn't even let The Retreat's shed get out of control, does he?"

Dale grinned. "Less of your cheek, brat. I'm pretty sure Luke wouldn't be averse to giving you a sound spanking should the occasion arise."

"Would *you*?" Zac's face was getting pinker. "Be averse, I mean."

"I hope you're not thinking about playing around today in order to get punished. I don't appreciate that kind of manipulative behavior, and most Doms won't stand for it."

Zac scuffed a foot on the floor. "I wouldn't do that. I don't want to waste your time. Call it naïve curiosity."

"You've never been spanked?"

Zac shook his head. "No, but it's something I…I dream about." His voice faded to a whisper—all confidence gone.

"Then to answer your question, I do enjoy delivering a sound spanking to a willing participant. I suspect it wouldn't be much of a punishment for you, though, so I'd have to think up something much more unpleasant. And don't ask me to tell you what that might be. Hopefully, wondering about it will be enough of a disincentive."

"I wonder if any of the Doms I'll be playing with will spank me." Zac seemed to be talking to himself rather than asking a question.

"Only if you agree to it. Remember that. I know you're here to learn and have new experiences, but you don't have to do anything you don't want to. Any of those Doms cross the line, and you go straight to Luke, okay? And if he's not around, you talk to Tor or to me."

"I'm not scared. I know how to look after myself."

"It's not about fear. In my experience, Zac, fresh submissives can be reticent about using their safe words because they're afraid that it makes them seem weak. They couldn't be more wrong. Doms aren't mind readers, we can't see inside your head, and not everyone is good at reading body language. Doms are human and even the best can get carried away in the moment. When endorphins take over, common sense takes a backseat. But to a good Dom, a safe word is sacrosanct. It'll break through a euphoric haze better than anything."

"I'll remember. Thanks, Si… Dale."

Smiling inside at the near slip, Dale handed Zac a pair of sturdy work gloves. "Here, put these on. They should stop you getting blisters or splinters when we're handling wood and clearing any thorny plants." His own favorite gloves were tucked into his back pocket. Warm and comfortable, the leather had grown supple over the years. Just for a moment he allowed himself to imagine what it might be like to deliver a spanking to Zac's bare behind wearing those gloves. He shook his head. He was far too old to be daydreaming on the job.

Zac was giving him a curious look, and Dale turned away, pretending to locate the tools they needed, even though he knew exactly where they were. "First job today is to clear the ground where we're building the beds. You take these." He handed Zac a hoe and spade and took an edging blade, some wooden pegs and string for himself. "There's a wheelbarrow around the back of the shed, we'll need that too, to clear away what we dig up."

As he squeezed past Zac to get to the door, their hips brushed, and Zac gave a small sigh. Dale didn't dare meet his gaze. *He's not for me. Get that into your thick head, Dale.*

While they walked back toward the kitchen garden, Dale kept clear air between them and decided that small talk might be the safest option. "I guess you've been to England before?" He sucked in a sharp breath as Zac almost tripped over the hoe but swung it out of the way of his feet at the last moment.

"Almost every year, since I was quite small. A whole two years once. Dad travels a lot on business, and he always tried to take me with him if it didn't clash with school. He often came over here in the summer to avoid the worst of the bad weather. You guys have a serious amount of rain—not that I noticed it letting up much in the summer some years."

"It's a trade-off for all the green." Dale gestured around him.

"And well worth it. Home for me most of the time is Arizona. The desert has its unique kind of beauty, but this is a special part of the world. We were mainly in London of course but tried to fit in visits to different places every time we were here. I really enjoyed Bath, and York. I like the old places best. Some of your cities give you that feeling of history surrounding you, like they've absorbed the past."

"I live in London, but I've been thinking of moving out to the sticks. Clients with the most to spend tend to be in the capital, but money isn't everything."

"No, it definitely isn't." Zac's tone was surprisingly vehement, and Dale belatedly remembered that he was talking to somebody for whom wealth was an immense burden. They went the rest of the way in silence, Dale kicking himself for being so insensitive.

"Could you talk me through what we're going to do today?" Zac asked. "I find it easier to be helpful if I know what I'm doing. I don't want to get in your way."

"You're a biologist, so you must know why raised beds can be useful."

"Well, they improve drainage and increase the soil temperature. They can enhance root health of the plants, especially if they're enriched with fertilizer or organic stuff. I guess if you want to grow something that doesn't like the natural soil here like lime-hating plants, they'd be good for that too."

"All good points. They're also a lot more accessible for people with mobility problems. Tor tells me he's had assistant chefs on occasion who use wheelchairs or who have arthritis, so we need to make sure the pathways between the beds are wide enough to wheel a barrow or accommodate a wheelchair, and they shouldn't be so wide that you can't lean to the middle from the edge because it's best not to walk around in them."

"I didn't think of that."

"We need to clear the site we're using of the existing vegetation and level it first. Then we'll mark out the beds with stakes and string and check the levels. That'll take us most of the day. I have a load of recycled pallets to build the sides from and then it'll be a case of filling them with a mixture of compost from the heap and some fresh topsoil. Depending on how it feels, I might mix in a bit of sand too."

"What about planting?"

"That'll be down to the usual gardening team, when they come back. The beds need to settle for two weeks before putting anything in them."

"You won't be here to do that then?"

"I'm filling in for two weeks while the usual grounds staff are taking a break."

"That's because of me, isn't it?" Zac frowned.

"Luke wanted to keep the staff to a minimum while you're here, yes." Dale wasn't going to lie. "The fewer people coming in and out, the easier it is to keep an eye on security. I'm doing Carey Hoffman a favor."

"I hope everyone knows how grateful I am about how much trouble they're going to for me."

"This is a business," Dale said. "A business that runs on its reputation amongst a very select clientele. They bend over backward for everyone who comes here, not just you, and I'm very happy to be contributing to such a fantastic garden."

"Are you saying I'm not special?" Zac gave Dale a cheeky grin.

"A special pain in the ass. Time to get to work, brat. Paying guest or not, as far as I'm concerned you've agreed to be my slave for the day."

Zac swallowed and made a subtle adjustment to his crotch that Dale couldn't fail to see. He looked heavenward. He wasn't in any way a religious man, but a bit of divine intervention wouldn't go amiss. *Lord save me from beautiful, feisty submissives.* He grabbed the spade and started to dig. Hard labor had to be the solution to thinking about how it might feel to have Zac's soft lips wrapped around his hardening cock.

"While I dig, you clear the weeds and roots into the barrow."

"Yes, Sir." This time Zac didn't try to correct himself.

Chapter Six

That evening, Zac lay soaking in a deep bath, the water scented and full of bubbles. He'd filled it up to his neck, ensuring that every protesting muscle was enveloped in warmth. Dale had shown no mercy, driving him hard, and Zac had used parts of his body that were unaccustomed to such physical exertion. He didn't want to be so sore the next day that he couldn't kneel for his first visiting Dom, so the bath was a necessity.

Despite the aches and pains, he had thoroughly enjoyed the hard labor. They'd made enough progress that he'd been able to help Dale build the walls of the first of three new raised beds. It had been incredibly satisfying to see fresh ground exposed, cleared of undergrowth, then the raised bed take shape. Filling it with rich, dark soil had been fun, and he'd had a worm counting competition with Dale. Even more satisfying had been Dale's praise, which warmed Zac from the inside out. Though he'd be otherwise engaged for the next two days, he'd promised Dale that in the break between Doms he would come to help again.

Zac closed his eyes, and his mind filled with the image of Dale's muscles flexing as he moved. Zac may have been tired but it didn't stop his cock jerking into action. He reached beneath the water and took it in a loose grip. *If I belonged to Dale, I wonder if he'd let me come. I'll bet he's into chastity.* That thought didn't help at all. Zac raised his hips so that his dick was no longer submerged. Slick with suds from the bath, it was the work of a moment to entice an orgasm. Not that his body needed much convincing. He'd been on edge all day so when he came, the pleasure was tinged with relief. Dale was handsome, strong and bossy — a complete erection-inspiring package as far as Zac was concerned.

He rose from the water then had a quick rinse with the shower attachment. It was at times like this that he could really appreciate the attention to detail at The Retreat. The towels were soft and fluffy, the bathroom the perfect temperature. The high-quality toiletries were plentiful. Wrapped in his towel, he padded through to the bedroom to grab a bottle of water from the fridge. A few long swallows of the icy cold liquid counteracted the heat from the water he'd been submerged in. "I might have had that bath a little too hot," he muttered. Feeling a bit lightheaded, he sat on the edge of the bed fanning his face. The knock at the door was so quiet he almost missed it.

"Come in!"

Skye's silver head appeared around the door, followed by the rest of him. He was carrying a tray and nudged the door closed with his backside.

"Oh, I can come back!"

"Why?"

"You're wearing a towel and you're wet?"

"I don't mind if you don't. Give me half a minute to get dry. Take the weight off, Skye."

"Are you sure? I brought soup for your supper."

Zac's stomach rumbled and he gave a wry grin. "It sounds like your timing is perfect." He pulled soft pajama bottoms and a T-shirt from the case he hadn't yet unpacked then retreated to the bathroom. "Have you eaten yet?" He raised his voice enough that Skye would hear him.

"I had my meal with the others, but Tor said you'd opted to have something in your room so I asked if I could bring it up. I thought... Well, I thought you might like somebody to talk to."

Zac emerged from the bathroom, toweling the drips from his hair. "I'd love for you to stay, if you can. Do you have to get permission from Luke or anything?"

Skye gave him a gentle smile. "He knows I'm here. He likes to know where I am all the time but he would never stop me from doing something I wanted to do. He likes to be in control, but he's not controlling. Does that make sense?"

"It does. It must be wonderful to know that somebody cares about you that much."

Skye blushed. "It's amazing."

"One day I want you to tell me all about how you and Luke got together." Zac clambered onto the bed, moved the pillows into two stacks before sitting against one of them. He patted the mattress. Skye put the tray between them and came to join him after kicking off his shoes.

"When we have more time. You need to eat. There's a terrine of soup, cauliflower, it's my favorite. Crusty bread, that Tor made fresh today, and then there's a slice of chocolate cake. Rayne made that, under supervision, but I've had a piece and I can testify to its yumminess."

If his complaining stomach wasn't enough, Zac soon realized how hungry he was once he started eating. The soup and bread were delicious and comforting. "I'm going to have to start taking advantage of the gym and the pool if Tor keeps feeding me this well."

"You're not the first guest, or member of staff, to say that and you won't be the last," Skye said. "Tor works magic in the kitchen. I can't resist anything he cooks so I try to eat smaller portions. Mind you, we all expend quite a lot of energy working here, there's so much to do and the place is big."

"You're very lucky to live here. It's a beautiful part of the world."

"I'd be happy to live anywhere providing I was with Luke. People matter more than place, don't you think?"

"You're right of course. I sometimes wonder what it would be like if Dad lost everything overnight, and we weren't ridiculously wealthy. Then I think about how much good he does, and how many people his philanthropy helps. Dad isn't his money. He's genuinely a good person. I hope he's passed that trait onto me."

"Well, I like you. Believe me, that doesn't apply to everyone who stays here. The majority of guests are great, but we get our share of visitors who aren't so nice."

"You must meet all kinds of interesting people."

"We do. I mean, I don't meet them all because I don't work here full-time but if The Retreat has taught me anything, it's to never take anyone at face value.

Stereotypes aren't real. We get Doms and subs in all shapes and sizes, all races and religions. Of course, this place isn't cheap so to some extent people who stay here are privileged, but I've learned a lot. Every now and again Carey pays for a group to come for the weekend from his club, people who wouldn't otherwise be able to afford it. Those weekends are huge fun because they all want to take advantage of every minute. The dungeon is always super busy."

"Oh God, I forgot about the dungeon. I wonder how hard-core my first Dom is going to be."

"You're not scared are you? The dungeon is full of fun times."

"The problem is that I have this idea about the kind of things I'm going to like but I've never experienced any of them. What if I don't enjoy any of it? What if I have a major freak out? That would be so embarrassing. When I was younger I longed to go scuba diving but when I got the chance—on the Barrier Reef would you believe—I got dreadful vertigo and had to surface. I'm afraid this'll be the same."

"You had a signal to go to the surface, right? That's what your safe word is for and don't forget that good Doms, as a rule, are all about making submissives happy. They want us to feel safe and secure and to have a good time. Carey wouldn't send anyone here to be with you unless they were a good Dom, so remember that, even though they can come across as all stern and strict, on the inside they're squishy teddy bears when it comes to us. I don't know how they do it. Being a Dom must be hard. They take charge of everything, take all the responsibility on their shoulders, make difficult decisions... So much scarier than anything in the dungeon." He tilted his head to one side. "Except the room with the medical kink stuff. No way am I going near those stirrups."

Zac snorted with laughter. "The whole being in charge thing is probably why I had no desire to follow my father into the business. I've helped him out a few times and he would have let me, if I worked my way up from an entry-level position but I don't think I'd have progressed. The mailroom sounds kinda fun."

"I don't mind making decisions in certain situations. You should meet my boss. She's a scatty professor and needs me to organize her or she'd never get anything done. I have to get a bit Dommy when I'm trying to get her somewhere on time."

"Other people are different. Making decisions about me isn't so easy."

"Luke is really good at that. If I have a problem, he'll help me work out the pros and cons and give me guidance if I need it. But he never forces a decision on me, it's me that makes it unless I beg him to decide for me. Begging can be fun."

"I think you're getting a little off track, Skye." Zac grinned. He polished off his slice of cake and shifted the crockery laden tray onto a side table so that he could lie back on the bed.

"That tends to happen whenever Luke gets into my head. I'm sorry."

"Don't be. I'm envious of what the two of you have together."

"I'm very, very lucky. Luke gives me exactly what I need. Carey does the same for Alistair, even though they're very different from us, and I know a few other committed couples who work for even more odd reasons. I really hope you find the man for you."

Zac's mind immediately went to a certain hot gardener. "I hope so too. At least this fortnight will help give me an idea of what it is I'm looking for."

"I should go." Skye began to wriggle off the bed.

"Can you stay?" Zac didn't want to be alone, and he really liked Skye. He was a gentle soul, kind and reassuring. "We could snuggle under the comforter, watch a movie… Only if you don't have any plans, that is."

"I'd love to. I'll take the tray down to the kitchen and let Luke know where I'm going to be, then I'll be back. Would you like some of Tor's special hot chocolate? Say yes, because then I have an excuse to have some too, and he uses whipped cream and marshmallows and real chocolate."

"Chocolate is my downfall, which you may have spotted when I made that slice of cake disappear. Yes, that sounds wonderful. Any preferences for a movie?"

"Something with a hunky leading man, of course."

"Of course."

Zac smiled as he flicked through the satellite channels on the TV looking for a film that they both might like. He needed to get into the right headspace for the coming days and a bit of mindless entertainment with a new friend would be the perfect way to spend a few hours. He couldn't deny that there was a kernel of anxiety in his gut, but he didn't feel like a boy scout had been practicing knots with his intestines. It was natural to be nervous about meeting a Dom for the first time, not knowing anything about him or his expectations, exploring the world Zac had dreamed about for so long. *It's what I want. What I need.* He wasn't tired enough to sleep yet and what he didn't need was to be left alone with his thoughts because they were a bit too concerned with Dale. He decided on a James Bond movie. A good dose of Daniel Craig hotness should steer him away from dreams of gardeners, however gorgeous they might be.

The bedroom door wasn't locked, and this time Skye slipped inside without knocking. He had changed his clothes and was wearing checked pajama bottoms and a Cambridge University hoodie. He was clutching two steaming mugs, which Zac assumed held Tor's miraculous hot chocolate. Skye handed Zac one of the mugs then scrambled beneath the covers, taking care not to tilt his drink.

"Luke thought this was a great idea. He said I could stay as long as I wanted but he doesn't really want to have to come in here and carry me out if I fall asleep, so you need to keep me awake, okay?"

"James Bond will make sure you don't doze off. Too noisy." Zac sipped his chocolate. "Wow, this is as good as you said. Thank you for doing this with me. I really appreciate it."

Skye leaned against him. "This is a treat for me. I tried having a film night with Rayne once and he was hopeless, commentated the whole time. I swear he never stops talking. If he and Tor ever get together properly, Tor's going to have to invest in a whole collection of gags."

"I love how you can say that without even thinking about it. It's amazing to be surrounded by people who know where I'm coming from."

"Talking of, did you have a good day in the garden with Dale?" Skye gave him a side eye.

"It was hard work but satisfying."

"He's very good-looking."

"Do you have to say things like that?" Zac fidgeted.

"It's an observation, that's all. He's not my type, but I can appreciate his appeal."

"There's something about him "

"There is, isn't there? You can tell he's a Dom from a mile away. Those tattoos are spectacular too. I guess he got his muscles from hard work rather than the gym."

This was not the direction Zac wanted their conversation to take, he was having enough trouble getting Dale out of his head. "Let's watch the film, shall we?"

Skye's expression was all innocence, but Zac wasn't falling for it. He shook his head. "Gardeners and gardening are a banned topic."

"Even Adam Smallmire?"

"Adam who?"

"He's a TV gardener here. Never mind, he's not fantasy material, unlike…"

"Skye!"

Skye blinked. "James Bond it is then." He settled back against his pillow pile with a satisfied smirk.

Zac shook his head and jabbed at the remote. "Everyone told me you were sweet and innocent."

"I am!"

"Are not."

"Am!"

"Film."

"Deal."

* * * *

When Zac awoke the next morning, it took him a moment to remember where he was but soon everything came flooding back. He'd had a wonderful evening with Skye, who'd left much later than he'd intended when Luke had shown up at the door to extract him. Zac had apologized but hadn't really meant it. He'd enjoyed Skye's company very much and had definitely made a friend for life. Once the film had started, they'd kept conversation to a minimum, but Zac had found a lot of comfort in Skye's undemanding presence. Now, as he lay in bed staring at the ceiling, his nerves returned. There was no way he was going to be able to eat breakfast.

He got up then spent a while in the bathroom cleaning out those parts of him that might be about to get a lot of attention. In the contract he'd signed, he'd agreed to the use of various toys, restraints and implements. He wanted to be prepared. He showered, shaved then dried his hair with more care than he usually would. His first Dom hadn't specified what he should wear so he picked a pair of comfortable jeans and a dark green shirt. He wasn't sure about footwear so opted for a pair of navy Vans, slipping them onto bare feet. The room phone rang so he picked up the handset.

"Hi, this is Zac."

"Good morning, Zac. I hope I didn't wake you."

"Hi, Rayne. No, I was up. No way was I going to sleep in this morning."

"I'm sure. Are you excited?"

"Can we settle on nervous anticipation?"

"I guess so. Tor asked me to call to see if you want any breakfast?"

"I don't think my stomach can deal with food this morning, but I'd love a cup of coffee if there's one going."

"Of course there is. Would you like it in your room?"

"No, I'll come down."

"Well, it's a cold morning and the fire's lit in the banqueting hall. I'll bring it in there for you."

"Sounds perfect, thank you." Zac replaced the receiver then headed downstairs. He needed something other than his room to look at for a while. He wasn't sure what time his first Dom would be arriving, and his nerves would only get worse if he stayed where it was. He passed Skye on the balcony, arms laden with bedding.

"Hey, Zac, good luck for today, not that you'll need it. I'm on my way to change your bed."

"I'd be happy to do that myself." Zac felt guilty that his new friend would be picking up after him.

"Rayne said you were on your way down for coffee so you go. This is my job, and I don't mind at all. I enjoy looking after people. Besides, you'll be doing it while the Doms are here."

"If you're sure you don't mind." The allure of coffee was enough to assuage Zac's guilt, so he continued to the banqueting hall where Rayne was putting a coffee pot on a low table near the fire. The room was huge and there was a noticeable change in temperature as Zac approached the fire.

"This is a toasty spot. Thanks, Rayne."

"No problem. I'd join you but if I don't get back to the kitchen, Tor will find new ways to torture me. Not that I don't enjoy that kind of thing, but I don't want to make it too easy for him."

Zac laughed. "I think you're setting a bad example."

"I do hope so. That second cup is for Luke by the way, he said to let you know he'd be joining you shortly."

"Thanks."

"Are you sure you don't want anything to eat? Not even some plain toast?"

"No, thanks. My stomach's performing some kind of acrobatic routine at the moment."

"Aw, once your Dom gets here, you'll feel better, I'm sure. Have a great day." While Rayne headed back to the kitchen, Zac stared into the flames, hands wrapped around his cup. The coffee was smooth and aromatic, just the way he liked it, but he decided to limit himself to one cup. He was so lost in his thoughts that he didn't notice Luke's arrival until he sat in the chair next to him and began pouring himself a coffee from the pot.

"How are you feeling this morning, Zac?"

"Fine, a little nervous but it's an excited kind of nervous if that makes sense?"

"Understandable, but I want to assure you again that you're completely safe here. What you're doing isn't easy and nothing happens that you don't want to. Your first Dom's name is Marcus and that's what he'd like you to call him rather than Sir or Master. He'll be here within the hour. I'm sure he'll spend some time getting to know you because even though he's seen your file, it's not the same as talking face-to-face."

"Do you know him?"

"I don't, but Carey speaks very highly of him. If at any time he opts to take you into the dungeon, I'll be acting as dungeon master. Do you understand what that means?"

Zac shook his head. "Not really."

"Well, in this case it means I'll be observing, either in the room or from close by. All the visiting Doms have agreed to this. It's a safety feature we prefer to use with inexperienced submissives like yourself. Any signs of distress, and I can be helpful in bringing things to the attention of the Dom, who may not always have his attention entirely on you, if he's setting up equipment for example. If I'm doing my job right, you won't even notice I'm there."

"That's reassuring."

"I'm not expecting anything to happen that I need to intervene in. These are experienced Doms and good men. They've seen the contract you signed and what you are and aren't prepared to do with them, but remember that it is entirely your prerogative to change your mind."

"Okay."

"We are all here for you. If you have any concerns at all, talk to me or Tor, or even Dale. You can also ask Rayne or Skye to come fetch one of us. We want you to have the best possible experience. I know it's easy for me to say but try to relax and enjoy it. Don't worry too much about what the Dom is thinking, or about trying to anticipate them. They'll issue clear instructions. They know that you have little experience and they won't be expecting perfection."

"That's good because I won't be anywhere close to that."

"No sub is perfect, even those that have been in the lifestyle for a long time. Honing the connection between two men is part of the pleasure."

"Just being around you and Skye is teaching me a lot."

"I'm glad. Skye was very eager that the two of you be friends. He really enjoyed spending yesterday evening with you."

"I had a good time too. He's a great listener."

"That he is." Luke put his cup down on the table then got to his feet. "I think I hear the sound of a car coming down the drive. I suggest you head to the front door to greet your Dom."

Zac was proud that he could put his cup down rather than dropping it. He managed a small smile for Luke before heading toward the door, and if his hands were shaking, he put that down to the chill away from the fire.

Chapter Seven

Zac went out into the front porch and took deep breaths of cool, crisp air. *When Dad suggested I take up meditation that time, I should have listened.* A sleek black sports car swung into the parking area. Zac didn't recognize the model until it got closer, and he could make out the Porsche badge. He stood with his hands clasped behind his back, his fingers intertwined so tightly they ached. He tried to relax his shoulders and affect a semblance of calm as the Porsche's driver reversed to one side. There was no rushing, no spitting of gravel, just a smooth maneuver before the low rumble of the engine shut off. Zac held his breath for the few seconds it took the driver to climb out of the vehicle. He had no idea what to expect but the man who approached him had a friendly, open smile. It was the first thing Zac noticed and it allowed him to release his breath.

"You must be Zac. I'm Marcus Coulter and I'm very pleased to meet you."

Marcus was about the same height as Zac. He was quite slim, wearing well-fitted navy trousers and a cream cable-knit sweater. He removed his sunglasses to reveal a pair of kind, golden brown eyes that matched his wavy hair. His skin was lightly tanned and laughter lines at the corner of his eyes told Zac that he was probably in his late thirties or early forties. Zac found he was reassured that Marcus was likely a very experienced Dom. He made a very good first impression.

"Good morning, Marcus. I hope you had good drive? I guess it must have been in that beautiful car."

"She's a self-indulgence I enjoy, I must admit. I work in the city and live in central London, so I don't get the chance to give her a good run very often. Coming down here this morning has been a pleasure."

"Can I help with your bag?"

"It's in the passenger seat, how about I show you my baby before we go inside?"

Zac had thought that the car was black but when he got closer, he could see that it was midnight blue and there was a slight sparkle to the paintwork. The interior was cream leather, and it didn't just *look* luxurious, it smelled that way too.

"She's gorgeous, but I still can't get used to how you guys all drive stick shifts over here."

"I tried an automatic once," Marcus said. "I didn't feel like I had enough control." His tone was mild but there was meaning in that word that had nothing to do with driving and it sent a shiver of anticipation down Zac's spine. He picked up Marcus' leather holdall then stood back from the vehicle.

"It's a beautiful car, but I think I'd be afraid to drive it."

"It's like everything—once you're used to her, she's easy enough to handle." Marcus locked the vehicle. "Let's go in, shall we?"

Zac led the way into the hall. "Would you like to go up to our room first, or I could show you around?"

"Let's find somewhere comfortable to sit and have a chat. I would kill for a mug of tea."

"Oh, I should have thought of that. Sorry."

"Zac, if I were in your shoes I'd be so terrified right now I wouldn't be able to breathe let alone think about refreshments. You're doing fine."

Zac gave a sigh of relief, grateful for Marcus' perception. "I'll leave your bag here for now. There are some really nice spots in the banqueting hall and the fire is going, which is cozy, even though it's an enormous room."

"Sounds perfect. You lead the way."

Zac was envious of Marcus' self-assurance but at the same time it eased his mind. He led Marcus to the same seats by the fire he and Luke had occupied earlier, and while Marcus settled, Zac went to the kitchen to ask Tor for some tea. Someone, probably Rayne, had already cleared the coffee pot and cups. Tor was there alone and told Zac to go back to Marcus and he would bring out refreshments. Zac returned to the hall to find Marcus sitting, legs stretched out and crossed at the ankles, a picture of relaxation.

"You may sit, Zac."

The order was a relief and circumvented Zac's need to hover rather than presume he should sit. He perched on the edge of his seat, hands folded in his lap. "Tea won't be long. The chef said he'd bring it out."

"Thank you, I'm parched. Have you got used to the British need for tea at every opportunity?"

Zac smiled. "I've been here many times over the years. You'll find I sometimes use British words, sometimes American or Canadian. I understand tea is sacrosanct and that dumping a load of it in a harbor did nothing for America's reputation. I'm Canadian, I think it's important to mention that."

Marcus chuckled. "Well, I know quite a lot about you Zac, because I've seen your file, so how about I tell you a little about me?"

"Yes, please."

"I can see you're nervous, and it's entirely understandable. I hope that once you get to know me you'll feel more relaxed. Nothing's going to happen over these two days that you don't consent to."

"I know, it's just a pretty strange situation."

"You'd know less about me if we hooked up on Grindr. Then you never know whether you'll be suited to a man you meet. Same if you go into a club and spot someone that appeals. Here, we have the advantage that people have been working away in the background to ensure that we'll get along."

"I hadn't thought of it like that."

They were interrupted briefly as Tor arrived with a pot of tea, a mug, milk jug and a plate of home-baked cookies on a tray. There was a glass of water for Zac. Other than saying hello to Marcus, Tor didn't engage in conversation and slipped away as quietly as he'd come once he laid everything out on the table.

"Somebody around here knows my weakness for pecans." Marcus took a cookie and crunched away. It was so normal that Zac found himself relaxing. "There, you already know something personal about me. I love pecans. I also support Harlequins rugby club, I can hold a tune and when time allows, I sing with a choir. I'm a commodities trader in the city, and I'm good at it. I've been a Dom as long as I can remember and active in the scene for the last twenty years."

"May I ask a question?" Zac wasn't sure if that was allowed.

"Ask as many as you like."

"Do you have partner, Marcus?"

"I don't. Sadly, I don't have time to bring a permanent submissive into my life. I work ridiculous hours and I would never be able to dedicate enough time and energy to him. There are several men at The Underground whom I play with on a regular basis, but I'm not exclusive with any of them."

"That's good, I mean good if that's the way you want it to be. I don't think I would feel comfortable even with the contractual restrictions in place for this arrangement if you had a partner."

"Neither would I, Zac. I must say that when Carey proposed this arrangement, I was intrigued. Your circumstances are unusual to say the least. I think this is a fine way for you to test the waters as it were. No two Doms are the same, as I'm sure you know."

"You're the fourth Dom I've met since I've been here," Zac said, "and I'm beginning to understand that there's infinite variety in the lifestyle and that applies to subs as well as Doms." He thought about how different Skye and Rayne were.

"That's very true. You'll find those of us with similar tastes, some who like delivering a whipping, true sadists who like nothing more than administering pain in a variety of ways, those who enjoy service, bondage or chastity... The list is endless."

"And just as many different submissives."

"Yes, Zac, exactly. It's no different from, say, rugby. There are obsessive fans who never miss a game, follow the players and know every score from every match since the founding of the club, and there are those like me who go along to the occasional home game with friends, usually followed by a drink somewhere to defrost. Then there's every shade in between." Marcus sipped his tea and gave Zac a contemplative look. "Do you know what kind of submissive you are yet, Zac?"

Zac examined his hands, still resting in his lap. "I'm still working it out. I want to please, I guess that's always been the case through school, with my father... If that's a need for validation then so be it. My father was always proud of me regardless, but I love the idea of taking care of someone and them in turn taking care of me." He gave a low chuckle. "But I also like the idea of being tied up, having my butt spanked, orgasm denial... I don't think I'll be heavily into pain but I haven't had a chance to find out yet. A whip seems...extreme, but I'm intrigued by the idea of a flogger or a paddle."

"I'm glad you're able to talk about it. The more you articulate, the more it helps me understand your needs. Some submissives find it impossible to express their own wishes and some Doms find pleasure in teasing out that kind of information. I prefer to start on more solid ground."

"If you don't mind me asking, Marcus, what kind of Dom are you?"

"Good question, though I'm not sure it's something I can answer and I'm not saying that to be obtuse. It's just that the kind of Dom I am has changed over the years. The things I enjoyed when I was twenty-one aren't the same as the things I enjoy now and I guess in another ten years they will have changed again. Domination for me is a fluid thing, not fixed, but at the moment I enjoy being with men who relish the exchange of power. Men who submit because they need to, not because they're playing some game fueled by what they've seen on the Internet. True submission is a gift, and I feel honored to receive it. I hope I can give any submissive I play with what he needs. I'm gay, I only play with men, which isn't necessarily true of all gay Dominants." He paused to sip his drink. "I enjoy using restraints, I like to know that my submissive is completely at my mercy and trusts me enough to put himself in that position. I want to give pleasure so if my submissive craves pain, I'm happy to deliver but I wouldn't call myself a sadist. I don't enjoy pain for pain's sake but if it gives a man erotic pleasure, that's fine. I like to bring a man to orgasm slowly, really slowly."

Zac noted the wicked gleam in Marcus' eye. Surreptitiously, he laid his hands in his lap to try and cover his arousal but of course Marcus noticed.

"It seems I've found one of your buttons, young man."

Zac ducked his head, heat blooming in his cheeks. "Maybe?"

"That's nothing to be ashamed of." Moving with deliberate care, Marcus put his mug back on the tray. "I think it could be time for you to show me our room now, don't you?"

Zac stood, his legs a little shaky. He couldn't help but wonder what Marcus had planned but there was no denying that Marcus' words had affected him.

Marcus led the way as they left the fireside and went back to the entrance hall. His overnight bag was nowhere to be seen. "I guess Skye has already been at work and taken your bag upstairs," Zac said. "That was nice of him."

"Carey told me this place was run with excellent efficiency," Marcus said, "everything I've seen so far attests to that. This staircase is spectacular." He ascended, brushing his hand along the smooth wooden banister.

"If you turn at the top, Marcus you'll get the best view of the stained-glass window." Zac joined him on the galleried landing and watched as Marcus took in the magnificent rose window.

"Breath-taking. Did you know that Carey and Alistair had to restore this place from the ground up? It was a complete ruin when they bought it, but they could see the potential."

"I didn't know that." Zac looked around with fresh eyes. "That must have been quite a project."

"They make an effort to employ people from within the lifestyle. A lot of excellent craftsmen worked around this place, and it shows. It's a sympathetic restoration. I imagine our room is just as appealing."

"Oh, yes. Sorry, Marcus." Zac walked across the landing to the door of the green room. "This is us." The door wasn't locked so he pushed it open, holding it while Marcus walked past him.

"This is impressive." Marcus moved around the room touching furniture and fabrics. He seemed to be a very tactile person. "I like the atmosphere. You can close the door, Zac."

"Sorry." Zac's face heated even more until he was convinced he must be the color of beetroot. He hadn't even noticed that he'd stood like a lemon, holding it open.

"You need to learn to stop apologizing," Marcus said. "The door stays unlocked. You can leave at any time. We're not going to do anything that you don't consent to."

Zac hung his head. "I'm so new to all this but I've wanted it badly for a long time. Now I'm here, you're here, and I've no idea what to do."

Marcus crossed the room. He tilted Zac's chin with one finger then gave him a gentle kiss on the cheek. "The easy answer is that you do what I tell you to. Your safe word is red, yes?"

"Yes, Marcus. Green for go, red for stop."

"I know this room holds some very kinky secrets, but I don't intend to do anything to scare you out of your wits."

"Thank you. I appreciate that." Zac thought that being told to close the drapes might be enough to freak him out at that moment. "Now, I want you to undress. You may keep your underwear on. Nothing else." Marcus retreated a few paces to sit in an armchair in the corner of the room. He was the epitome of relaxed control.

With trembling fingers, Zac removed his clothes, folding them into a pile at his feet. By the time he was finished and standing there dressed only in a black cotton jock, he was hard, his dick pushing against the soft fabric.

"Stand with your legs slightly apart and put your hands behind your head." Marcus' gentle tone became firmer. "You have a beautiful body, Zac."

"Thank you." Zac locked his knees to stop his legs shaking. He was hyper aware of the slight pull on his shoulders and the heat in his balls. He curled his toes, digging them into the carpet pile. When Marcus rose from his seat, Zac's breath hitched. Marcus didn't comment but came across the room in a few short strides.

"I'm going to touch you now. I want you to maintain this position."

How hard can it be? Zac sank his teeth into his lower lip, worrying the tender flesh as Marcus circled him. He stroked Zac's shoulders and biceps, then ran his fingers down Zac's spine until he reached the waistband of his jock. Zac was painfully aware of his exposed backside and wished he'd worn something with more coverage.

"I appreciate your choice of underwear. It displays you nicely." Marcus continued his slow circuits, his touch remaining soft and gentle, sometimes the barest brush of fingertips. He hadn't yet touched Zac's ass or cock, and Zac found that he desperately wanted him to. "Do you have any injuries I need to be aware of?" Marcus asked. "Bondage can put considerable strain on your joints, and I don't want to cause any damage."

"No, there's nothing. I broke my wrist as a kid, but it doesn't cause me any problems. I have a few scars from playing ice hockey, but I didn't keep it up long enough to cause myself any lasting injuries."

"An exciting sport to watch, though not exactly prolific in this country. There are a few teams, though I think a lot of our players are imported from Canada, Russia and the USA." As he spoke Marcus rubbed the back of his hand across one of Zac's nipples and he gasped. "Sensitive. Good to know." Zac took a few short, rapid breaths. "You may bring your hands down but keep them behind your back." Marcus went over to the bed and rolled back the covers. He eyed the four corner posts. "Ah, perfect." He pulled the restraints at each corner free. The clink of chains sent a shiver down

Zac's spine. Marcus patted the bed. "Come and lie down. Present your limbs to the cuffs."

Receiving an order was a relief. Zac found his head was clearer when he had a simple instruction to follow. He did as Marcus commanded, lying spread-eagled on the bed. He focused on remembering how to breathe while Marcus fastened his wrists and ankles into heavy steel cuffs.

"These cuffs are quite extreme, but the weight will keep them in your head," Marcus said. He walked around the bed adjusting the chains until Zac was stretched into a star shape. There was little play in the chains and the realization dawned that he was completely at Marcus' mercy. His cock twitched, apparently content with the situation. Zac shifted his hips, trying in vain to get some friction from cotton against skin.

"Be still." The snap of Marcus' voice was as efficient as a crop or cane would have been. Zac froze.

"You want to come, don't you, Zac?"

"Yes... Yes, Marcus."

"Well that's not going to happen for a long time." Marcus trailed his hand across Zac's groin.

"I thought you weren't a sadist!" Zac's voice betrayed his desperation.

"Not in the traditional sense of the word, no. But there's a difference between sadism and wanting to make you suffer."

"I'm not sure I understand differentiation."

"You don't need to understand. Remember, Zac, this is about your submissive need to give a Dominant pleasure. It's my pleasure not to let you come, however much you want to. I have to say, you present a stunning picture like this."

"Thank you, I think…"

Marcus laughed. "Perhaps you could direct me to the toy cupboard. I'm assuming they keep the rooms here well stocked."

"The chest next to the wall over there. I had a quick look inside, but it was a bit scary. I didn't know what most of the stuff was for."

Marcus went and opened it. "Goodness. I'm quite jealous. This makes my collection seem somewhat lacking. Everything here is of excellent quality."

From his position, Zac could only see Marcus' back, not what he was doing. A dozen different scenarios flashed through his mind, and he closed his eyes, trying not to let his imagination run away with him. When Marcus returned to the side of the bed, he was holding an implement Zac recognized.

"You know what this is?"

"A crop. I grew up with horses." Zac's mouth was dry, and it was hard to get the words out. "What are you going to do with it?"

In answer, Marcus laid the crop across Zac's chest, the leather square at the end resting on one nipple. "That's up to me, isn't it?"

"I… Yes, it is."

"Are you still at green, Zac?"

Zac thought about it. "I am. I don't understand why, but I am."

"And that's why I'm here, to help you understand what you need. How do the restraints make you feel?" Marcus stroked Zac's chest with the crop.

"Safe. Frustrated too, but it's a relief not to have to worry about what to do with my arms and legs. I just have to lie here and accept your decisions."

"And accept them because you want to, not for any other reason." Marcus slapped each nipple in turn with the crop. None of the blows were painful but the steady repetition built heat until Zac was desperate to twist away. He needed the crop to land somewhere else. Anywhere else. He whimpered. "Still green?" Marcus didn't stop.

"Green." Zac ground out the word. "Please!"

"You're not to come."

"That's not fair!" Zac wasn't sure he could come untouched, but the possibility was growing. Marcus paused then blew onto Zac's tormented nipples. "Aagh!" Zac lifted his hips from the bed and tugged at his restraints. He was right on the edge of orgasm, but not quite there. It was agonizing.

"Take a few deep breaths." Marcus held a bottle of water to Zac's lips then supported his head as he drank.

"Thank you." Zac was already shattered. Ready to come apart at the seams after such a short time. He stared as Marcus tipped a little of the icy water into his hands then rubbed them together. He smiled as he placed both palms across Zac's chest. Zac screamed as icy cold met burning heat and his over-sensitized nipples sent lightning bolts to his cock.

"You can have five minutes to recover," Marcus said. "Then we'll continue."

"Are you sure you're not a sadist, Marcus?" Zac said, desperate to reach for his aching shaft. He clenched his ass muscles, lifting his hips from the bed.

"Quite sure." Marcus' serene smile was at odds with the way he was smacking the crop into his palm. "You enjoyed that, didn't you?"

"I…" Zac didn't want to admit that he had.

"That's what I thought."

Chapter Eight

Dale had made decent progress with his gardening work, interspersing digging sessions with circuits of the grounds. So far his timing had worked out fine. Skye had brought him a cold drink at eleven along with a chocolate muffin and he'd stayed while Dale ate and drank, asking detailed questions about the best composting methods. Dale was more than happy to chat. He missed Zac's company, missed teasing him and testing his willingness to be obedient. Skye's submission might as well have been painted on his skin — Zac's was more difficult to decipher.

He'd been working for another two hours or so when Tor sent Rayne out to invite him in for lunch and he accepted. The sandwiches, fruit and Victoria sponge washed down with two mugs of tea were delicious and Dale relished every bite. Luke hadn't appeared for the meal and Dale wondered if he was acting as dungeon master for Marcus. The thought turned his stomach — Zac was far too inexperienced to be taken down there so soon. His concern was proved unneeded when Skye explained that Luke had driven into Lyndhurst for an optician's appointment. Dale was relieved but berated himself for filling his head space with matters that were none of his business.

Once Skye and Rayne were engaged with the washing up, Tor took the opportunity to let him know he was now in on Dale's secret and that he'd cover if any of the others asked questions regarding his whereabouts. He offered his help any time he was free, and Dale returned to the garden glad he'd gained more support.

Around three he left some tools strategically placed to appear as if he'd gone for a quick break and made his way back to his apartment. He showered then laid out a set of dark clothes. Thankful for the blackout blinds that kept the bedroom dim, he lay on the bed in his underwear. He set the alarm on his phone to wake him in four hours, though his inner body clock rarely failed him. He closed his eyes, blanked his mind and tried to sleep.

His army career had prepared him well for odd hours, and he had the enviable talent of being able to sleep anywhere, anytime. It was no hardship at all with a comfortable bed rather than the rock-hard ground or a camp bed. He slept well and woke rested two minutes before the alarm went off. He dressed before gathering some useful kit into a small backpack. Outside the light had almost gone but he managed to clear away his discarded tools without resorting to a torch. Thick cloud cover would make his job easier, but as he moved around he kept close to shrubs and trees from habit rather than a need to conceal himself.

The grounds were a whole different world after sunset. In places, the undergrowth was dense, and as

Dale made his way through, sensitive rodent ears sent animals scurrying. An owl hooted repeatedly from somewhere close, probably spotting dinner thanks to Dale's disturbance. The smell of the foliage and leaf litter was stronger, more acidic. Several of The Retreat's windows were illuminated, and Dale couldn't help but wonder what was going on inside. *Is Zac kneeling for Marcus? Has he used his safe word? Has he been flogged, spanked, plugged?* Dale gave a low growl of discontent then sighed. It wasn't his place to be unhappy about any of those possibilities. Marcus might be exactly what Zac needed.

Grumbling beneath his breath, Dale made his way toward the main gate to check for any sign of tampering. He pulled a pair of night vision goggles from his pack, putting them on once he was far enough from the house to make walking blind dangerous. After rounding a bend in the drive, he could no longer see the buildings when he looked back, and darkness closed around him. He kept walking until the wrought iron gates at the entrance to the property loomed in front of him. A fox crossed his path, pausing to give him a curious stare before going about its business, tail twitching.

There was no easy way to get through the gates without disturbing Luke, because they could only be opened from the house. Dale shifted his backpack into a better position then began to climb. The intricate ironwork had plenty of hand and footholds. It took some effort, but Dale cleared the top with only a couple of scratches for his trouble. He dropped to the ground, wincing as a twinge shot through his hip. His plan was to walk the perimeter, which was going to take a while. He adjusted his goggles then set off at a steady pace, scanning the ground for any sign of activity. Willpower alone kept his mind from straying to a certain young man.

Zac was struggling to hone his strength of will. He spotted movement outside from the small snug where Skye had set up a table for two. Marcus had requested a more intimate setting than the grand banqueting hall for their evening meal, and Zac had to agree that this room with its comfy armchairs, shelves of books and roaring fire was a good choice. They'd arrived five minutes earlier, and Zac had wandered across to the leaded window to check the view. There wasn't much to see as the light from the window didn't stretch very far, and beyond, the grounds were in darkness. He did spot movement, just a shadow and only for an instant, but he knew instinctively that it was Dale. It had been a struggle to keep Dale out of his head all day. The intensity of the scene with Marcus had helped but every now and again Zac had imagined Dale wielding the crop instead of Marcus.

"Dale's working late," he said, addressing his comments to no one in particular. Skye, who was putting the finishing touches to the dining table, came across to him.

"He said he likes to take a stroll in the evening, though I hope he has a torch or he'll be falling flat on his face. It's pitch black out there tonight."

"Who's Dale?" Marcus laid a hand on Zac's shoulder.

"The gardener," Skye replied. "He arrived at the same time as Zac. He's working on Tor's kitchen garden."

"I admire that talent," Marcus said. "I have trouble keeping a window box going."

Zac turned away from the window. Marcus deserved his attention. "I saw someone outside. The movement caught my eye."

Marcus steered him to the table, and Zac was glad there was no further interrogation. He was exhausted, and a bit lightheaded at the end of a day that had been full of revelations. After focusing on his chest for so long, Marcus had untied him then flipped him onto his belly and applied the crop to his ass with similar diligence. No single blow had ever hurt. Marcus was a master at layering heat until it blossomed into a deep ache that kept Zac hard and wanting.

Following a light lunch that Zac had eaten kneeling at Marcus' side, he'd been returned to his position on the bed, once again restrained face up. The first tap to his balls had shattered him. He could barely remember what happened from then on, recalling only his inability to focus on anything but his cock. Marcus had applied the crop to his shaft and balls over and over again. After a while he'd shoved a pillow beneath Zac's hips which had given him better access to the tender area behind Zac's balls. Zac would never forget the slap of leather against skin. Time and again Marcus had brought him to the point where he thought he could no longer hold back his orgasm but then Marcus would lay the crop down, give him sips of water, utter soothing words in his ear and the urge would subside a fraction. Always there, it became an itch Zac couldn't scratch. In the end it wasn't a blow that broke him, it was Marcus cupping his aching balls in a cool hand. Zac had come so hard he'd blacked out momentarily and when he'd awoken, he'd burst into tears, utterly rung out.

Marcus had untied him then covered him with a soft blanket while he'd run a bath. When Zac felt able to walk to the bathroom, Marcus sat on the edge of the tub while Zac soaked away the stress of the day. Marcus hadn't spoken but offered tender touches and care. He'd given Zac a few moments alone while he'd gone to stretch his legs and make arrangements for dinner. Zac had spent the time dissecting in his head what had happened and how it made him feel.

Now, in the warmth of the snug, watching Skye hum as he worked, Zac wondered if he had imagined the day. The sensitivity of various body parts rubbing against his clothing told him it had been real, but his memories were hazy. Marcus pulled out a chair for him, and he sat, doubtful that he'd be able to eat. Skye left the room, and Marcus joined him at the table. He poured him a glass of red wine, the dark liquid glinting like blood through the crystal.

"You've had time to process things a little, so how are you feeling?" Marcus asked.

Zac played with the stem of his wineglass. He took a small sip and the burst of flavor across his tongue seemed more vibrant than it should have. "I'm not sure. Dazed? Thank you for today Marcus. I never knew…"

"Should I take that as a good or bad thing?"

"Good. Definitely good. It's a bit overwhelming."

"Well, you're off the hook this evening. I want you to enjoy your drink, though I wouldn't recommend you have more than one. Then enjoy a nice meal with a new friend…because I hope we'll stay friends when this is over. I don't want you worrying about what I'm planning for the evening because I intend that we do nothing but have a restful night's sleep. I'm not making any promises about tomorrow, however." He raised his glass in a toast, and there was a mischievous glint in his eye.

"You're enjoying this, aren't you?" Zac couldn't help but smile.

"It was a wonderful day, Zac. I enjoyed myself very much. For someone with so little experience, you submitted beautifully and that gave me great pleasure."

"I don't think I was aware of what was going on half the time. I was hardly attentive to your needs."

"If that was what I wanted from you, the day would have been very different."

"Being helpless, handing over control... That was liberating."

The door swung open, and to Zac's surprise it was Luke who came in, carrying their starters. He put the plates in front of them.

"As you requested, Marcus, Tor has kept the menu light. I hope you both had a fulfilling day."

"It was remarkable," Marcus said. "Perhaps we could talk after dinner, Luke?"

Luke nodded. "And what about you Zac?"

"It was frustrating, tormenting, exhilarating... Marcus was incredible, Mr. Redding."

"I'm glad to hear it. Enjoy your meal, gentlemen. I wanted to check in, but Skye will be serving for the rest of the evening."

Once Zac started eating, he realized that he was hungry after all. The food was worthy of any high-class restaurant, and he enjoyed every mouthful. He stuck to a single glass of wine as Marcus suggested because, though it was delicious, he wanted to keep a clear head. Marcus kept conversation to a minimum, the topics undemanding. Skye's service was unobtrusive and efficient. By the end of the meal Zac was feeling a little less scattered, but his thoughts were still whirling in multiple directions.

"Would you mind if I went outside for a stroll, Marcus? I think I need to get some fresh air before bed."

"Of course. Strange as it sounds, I need to go through a debrief on our day with Luke. His insights on how I should approach tomorrow will be valuable. I'd suggest you don't stray too far from the building though."

"I won't. I need a bit of space around me for a while. I'll see you upstairs."

Marcus rose and pulled Zac's chair out for him. "Half an hour, no longer."

Zac left the main door of The Retreat ajar then strolled outside. The bite of the cold night air was like a hit of adrenaline, and he breathed deeply. He wasn't sure of the exact time, but it had to be close to midnight. He decided his best bet would be to follow the drive as walking without light would be least hazardous that way. Face-planting in the gravel was not on his to do list. He'd never minded darkness, he found it comforting. The sounds the nocturnal creatures made were very different from those in Arizona, and he couldn't help but smile as he spotted the fluffy tail of a rabbit disappearing under a bush. He stopped and stared up at the sky, but it was overcast and he couldn't see the stars. He wondered how different the constellations might look from here rather than from North America.

"You shouldn't be out here."

"Holy fuck!" Zac's heart pounded in his chest as Dale emerged from the darkness. His approach had been completely silent. "Give a guy some warning would you. You could have given me a heart attack." Dale's grin was disarming. "Why are you dressed like some kind of special forces ninja?" Zac took in Dale's all-black outfit, which he had to admit was super-hot.

"Ninja? Really? You watch way too many movies."

"Don't try to avoid the question."

"I like to walk in the dark and I have a lot of black clothes in my wardrobe. Satisfied, Mr. Curious?" Dale stepped closer, close enough that Zac could smell his aftershave. "I'll walk you back to the building. Does anyone know you're out here?"

"Marcus does."

"Ah, Marcus."

Zac didn't know what to make of Dale's tone, nor how to feel about Dale's hand on the small of his back. "It's been an interesting day. Exhausting."

"He didn't hurt you?"

"You know why he's here."

"Yes, but that doesn't mean he should be inflicting pain. Unless that's what you want."

"It isn't but no, he didn't hurt me. He was kind. A gentleman, and I know how to use a safe word."

"Will you be spending the day with him again tomorrow?"

"Yes, each Dom will be with me for two days. You sound annoyed." Zac leaned close to Dale's body until they were touching, arm to arm.

"I have no right to be. What you do here isn't my business."

Zac came to a halt then turned to face Dale. His features were cast in shadow. "Would you like it to be?"

"That's not a fair question, Zac." Dale moved his hand to the nape of Zac's neck before ruffling his hair.

"No, not fair. Selfish." It was hard to tell in the low light, but Zac thought he detected a hint of satisfaction in Dale's expression.

"You need to keep your attention on Marcus. Go inside. Sleep well."

Zac walked back to the house, knowing that Dale's eyes were on him until he went inside. As he stood at the base of the stairs, his hand strayed to his cock, which had perked into life in Dale's presence. Zac was about to share a bed with Marcus, and he felt desperately guilty for wishing that it could be Dale instead.

Chapter Nine

The next morning, Zac emerged from the bathroom feeling too big for his skin. Marcus had handed him an enema kit, asked if he needed any help then left him to it. Zac was relieved Marcus hadn't insisted on joining him because he couldn't imagine somebody watching while he carried out the task. Marcus had showered first and was already dressed in black jeans and a dark red fitted shirt.

"Leave the towel in the bathroom, Zac. You won't be getting dressed today."

Zac gulped. He wasn't especially bothered about being naked in front of Marcus but the dynamic of being bare while the other man was fully dressed brought a whole new atmosphere into the room. He returned to the bathroom to hang up the towel he'd been wearing then went back into the bedroom.

"You blush very nicely," Marcus observed. "I've ordered breakfast to be delivered here. First I want you to place your hands on the bed and bend over."

Zac did as he was told. "Have you played with toys before?" Marcus asked as he rose. Zac didn't want to confess to the close relationship he had with his toy collection, so he simply nodded. "I'm going to plug you. I wouldn't do that unless you'd had some experience." Marcus showed Zac a slender silver dildo. It was much smaller than the ones Zac was accustomed to using. He enjoyed the sensation of being stretched to the limit — something else he wasn't ready to confess. It had been a while, however, and when Marcus pressed the toy against Zac's hole, he tensed.

"I know this isn't the same as doing it to yourself. You need to relax. I don't want to hurt you." Marcus stroked Zac's backside while applying steady pressure. Zac forced himself to relax, and the dildo slipped inside him. His inner muscles immediately started working the invader, and he moaned. "Good. Stand up and turn around." Marcus proceeded to lock a cock ring around the base of Zac shaft. "I'm in a generous mood. You don't have permission to come, and this should make obedience a lot easier."

"Thank you, Marcus."

"Sarcasm will get you a spanking, young man." Marcus chuckled. "Take a seat, breakfast should be here any moment."

Zac scampered over to the table and took the seat facing the door because it was the one that made his nudity least visible. He couldn't decide whether his erection was caused by an exhibitionist streak he didn't know he had, the dildo that was pressing on all kinds of good places inside him or because Marcus had told him he couldn't come.

"How did you sleep?" Marcus asked as he went to answer a soft knock at the door.

How the hell does he expect me to engage in intelligent conversation? Zac shifted in his seat. He didn't see who had delivered breakfast because Marcus wheeled the trolley back into the room himself.

"I dreamed but I can only remember flashes. I woke a few times, so not that well. There was too much going on in my head, I suppose."

"If it all gets too much for you today, I want you to tell me." Marcus moved two covered plates from the trolley to the table. There was also a jug of orange juice, a plate of cut fruit, a silver rack of toast and a basket of pastries. Marcus left the coffeepot on the trolley. "I never saw the sense in messing around with fruit and cereal before the main event. Hot food first, then if you still have room there's plenty more." He resumed his seat at the table. Zac lifted the cover from his plate to find beautifully presented eggs Benedict.

"We *are* being spoiled."

"There's nothing wrong with an occasional treat, and we do have something to celebrate after all." Zac sipped orange juice and gave Marcus a quizzical look. "You survived your first full day as an out and proud submissive."

"I suppose I did." Zac clinked his glass against Marcus'. "Oh God, these eggs are amazing." Moaning his pleasure around every forkful, Zac consumed the food with gusto.

"How do you think you would cope with a Dominant who wanted to control your diet?"

"That's a thing?"

"For some. Some Doms like to control every aspect of their sub's life including what they eat and when. I'm not one of them."

"I'm grateful for that. I don't think that's something I'd appreciate, even for a short time. I like my food!"

"I don't think so either. What aspect of what we did yesterday did you enjoy the most?"

"I thought about it a lot, last night. The bondage was great, the edging not so much, though it was part of your control and that's what was best for me. Handing over control, being helpless, even though I know in reality I could have stopped it all at any time."

Marcus gave a slow smile. "I'd be surprised if edging was top of any submissive's wish list, but you handled it well. I was impressed. If I hadn't known, I would never have guessed you hadn't played seriously before and yes, that is a compliment."

Zac couldn't meet Marcus' eyes. "Thank you. I hope you had a good time too? I don't want this to be all about me."

"You don't need to worry on that score. I enjoyed yesterday very much and I intend to have just as good a time today."

Zac selected a few pieces of fruit. "Would you like me to pour you some coffee, Marcus?"

"Yes, please."

"How do you take it?"

"With a little more cream than is good for me."

Smiling, Zac poured two cups, added cream then returned to the table. The coffee proved to be as good as the food. Marcus was smiling and that made Zac happy. Serving him a cup of coffee had been a simple thing but satisfying.

"Have you had enough to eat?" Marcus asked, after a few minutes of companionable silence.

"Yes, thank you. Those pastries were melt-in-the-mouth, weren't they?"

"Better than any I've had, even in Paris. Tor is exceptionally talented. Put everything back on the trolley then we'll wheel it into the corridor."

Zac registered the slight change in Marcus' tone to something firmer. He did as he was told, praying that there wouldn't be anyone out on the gallery. His pulse had sped up a bit by the time he returned to the room.

"I want you to kneel, spread your legs apart, ass on your heels. Hands behind your back."

Zac did his best to get into position gracefully. Even though he'd been naked in Marcus' presence for a while, this felt like new, raw exposure. His cock was aching and hard, the gleam of pre-come glossing its tip.

Marcus rose then walked across to the toy box. "I intend to take you a little further today. I wouldn't do that if I didn't think you could take it. Are you at green?"

"Green, yes, Marcus." Zac took some long, slow breaths. He tracked Marcus as he delved into the box. "First, a blindfold." Marcus handed it to Zac. "Take a look." It wasn't a simple mask, or strip of fabric. Two leather ovals, lined with black fleece slid on a leather strap, which closed with a buckle. It was an ingenious design, which meant that the pieces to cover the eyes would be a perfect fit. Zac handed it back to Marcus who proceeded to fasten it in place.

"Hands behind your back again, please. You should never underestimate the power of a blindfold, Zac. With this in place you instantly become reliant on your other senses and your ability to trust me. The erotic energy of a scene escalates fast when you lose your sight." With the blindfold strapped in place, Zac was disoriented for a while and felt unbalanced, even though his position was stable. Marcus' voice became his anchor. "Is it comfortable? I want you to let me know if anything is digging in or pinching."

"It's fine." Zac wasn't yet sure if that was the truth. He was more thrown by this than anything Marcus had done the previous day. The darkness was absolute. The blindfold didn't admit the slightest glimmer of light.

"Good. Handcuffs next." The clink of chain proceeded the cool touch of metal around Zac's wrists. "This type will ratchet tighter if you struggle, so don't. I want you to keep still. Think about how you're feeling, consider your pleasure points. What do you like about this and what don't you?" Marcus rested his fingers on Zac's shoulder. "I'm going to be sitting in the chair in the corner, reading the newspaper. I'm old-fashioned, I still like to get newsprint on my skin. You should be able to maintain that position for some time but if anything starts going dead or tingling, let me know. Still green?" There was a whisper of air against Zac's skin as Marcus moved away.

"Yes, Marcus." Zac strained to follow Marcus' movements as he traversed the room, settled in his seat then opened the paper that had been delivered with breakfast.

"Remember, you should speak up if you get uncomfortable. I'm right here and I won't leave you."

Zac focused on keeping his balance. Spreading his knees wide helped with that, though not with his state of mind as he visualized the picture he presented, cock jutting from its steel collar. Sitting on his heels meant that there wasn't enough compression to cause his legs to go dead, but Zac felt the slight strain in his thigh muscles. Every now and again Marcus turned a page, and the rustle of paper broke the silence. Then, without warning, the toy in Zac's ass began to vibrate.

"Fuck!" He fought to maintain his position.

"Something wrong, Zac?"

"No, no... Fuck." Zac took several heaving breaths. Seemingly of its own volition, his body worked the dildo. The tip vibrated against his prostate sending waves of stimulation through his body. "Marcus... Please!" As suddenly as they'd started, the vibrations stopped. "Oh, thank God." Zac had no doubt that his orgasm had only been held at bay by the cock ring, and he wasn't convinced that it would necessarily stop him from coming if Marcus activated the device again. It was all Zac could think about. The anticipation, the expectation that those sensations would come again was all consuming. His lack of sight had seemed to magnify his sensitivity a thousandfold.

"I think I'll attempt the crossword, next. Are you any good at solving cryptic clues, Zac?"

"You are... That's... Unbelievable."

"Are you not into word puzzles?"

"No, I mean yes I am but at this moment... I can't think. Please, Marcus, I need to come."

"No. What you need to do is suffer for my enjoyment."

Zac gritted his teeth. Marcus sounded so certain of his ability to command.

"Here's a good one, considering the circumstances. Five letters, Furious, Mark voted wrong."

Zac wanted to scream. "How can you expect me to think about it?"

"The answer is cross. Quite a simple one. Are you cross with me, Zac?"

Before Zac could answer, the plug began to vibrate again. He pressed his lips together, determined not to give Marcus the pleasure of hearing him scream because he knew deep down that the sound would make Marcus smile. Zac might be blindfolded but he could visualize.

"It's quite a conundrum, isn't it? A bit like this crossword puzzle. You want to come, but you can't because I won't allow it. You probably want to beg, even though you know it won't do you any good. You want me to turn off the vibrations, but you won't ask, and all the while I'm watching you come apart and it's turning me on like you wouldn't believe."

The vibrations stopped. Behind the blindfold, Zac's eyes were wet with tears. Marcus' words were far too close to the truth for comfort. Zac's safe word hovered on the tip of his tongue, but he wouldn't use it. Not for this. He wasn't in pain. Marcus wasn't damaging him. To use his safe word now would be petulant. "You're an utter bastard, aren't you?"

"I'm surprised you didn't work that out yesterday." Marcus' tone told Zac that he *was* smiling.

Perspiration slicked Zac's skin. It crossed his mind that his mouth was dry and at that moment, Marcus pressed the neck of a bottle to his lips. "Take a drink." Zac sucked desperately at the bottle, the cool liquid soothing the throat he only now realized he had strained.

"It's polite to thank your Dominant for refreshment."

"Thank you, Marcus." The words were broken glass on Zac's tongue.

Marcus returned to his seat, and the paper rustled once more. Every now and again he would mutter a clue but didn't appear to expect Zac to make any contribution to solving it. The dildo stayed dormant for a long time, and Zac was on the point of relaxing when it went off again. This time he did scream. He was so focused on his need to come that he didn't realize Marcus had moved until the Dom wrapped his hand around Zac's shaft. The vibrator was still going, and Zac would have done anything to escape the torment.

"You want to come, don't you, Zac?"

What a fucking ridiculous question. "You know I do!"

"Say please."

"Please, please let me come, Marcus."

"You have permission."

In the next minute, Zac learned that he was not one of those men who could come while wearing a heavy cock ring. He struggled, frantically working the vibrator, moving so much that the cuffs tightened around his wrists.

"Interesting." Then Marcus was touching him, removing the ring. Zac came with agonizing force, and Marcus helped him along, squeezing and tugging his dick until he was milked dry. Zac gasped for air, overwhelmed by the intensity of his orgasm. This toy was still vibrating, his inner muscles trying to pull it deeper. Then it was over. The vibrations stopped, and he sagged forward, exhausted. Marcus wound his fingers into Zac's hair and held him upright. "Kneel up. I'm going to take the vibrator out."

When it was gone, Zac could only describe how he felt as bereft. He was so empty, he wanted to cry. Marcus gave him more water then removed the handcuffs but not the blindfold. He helped him onto the bed before rubbing him down with a soft towel. Zac was limp, he could do nothing to assist and didn't want to. He needed Marcus to take care of him.

Marcus whispered soothing words as he provided after-care following the scene. He pulled the covers over Zac's body. "Rest now. Have a nap. I'll be right here."

"Don't leave me." Zac was ashamed of being so needy.

"Of course not. I'm not going anywhere. But I do have a crossword to finish."

Zac was glad of the blindfold because otherwise Marcus would have seen him rolling his eyes. A nap was an order Zac was happy to follow. He was warm and comfortable, no longer in fear of the vibrator, he was able to relax and soon drifted off.

* * * *

"Oh, how long have I've been asleep?" Zac sat up in bed and stretched. The blindfold had gone but the curtains were drawn, keeping the room dim. He blinked, trying to focus.

"Just shy of two hours." Marcus put down the book he'd been reading then walked across to the side of the bed. "How are you feeling?"

"Good, actually," Zac admitted, a little surprised. "I can't believe I slept for two hours in the middle of the day."

"It's not unusual. An intense scene can be exhausting. Does anything hurt?"

Zac took a moment to consider. He rubbed at his wrists. "No, a little dented perhaps."

"If you're feeling up to it, take a shower then we'll go downstairs for lunch. If I keep you shut away in here much longer, Luke will be banging on the door to check on you."

A shower sounded great, as did escaping Marcus' scrutiny to get his thoughts in order. Zac slipped from beneath the covers then padded through to the bathroom.

"Leave the door open."

Zac paused, then shrugged. Doms liked to be in control and apparently that extended to whether or not he got any privacy. The shower was welcome, but he didn't hang around and this time, after drying off, he went back into the bedroom naked.

"Am I allowed to dress, Marcus?"

"Tempting though it is to lead you around like that, yes, you may dress. You should realize that might not always be the case. Some Doms like to keep their subs naked all the time when they're at home and at BDSM clubs and events. It's not an uncommon sight at Carey's club."

"Why the aversion to clothing?" Zac asked as he pulled on jeans and a soft black pullover.

"It's a form of control. It means you have nowhere to hide and allows easy access to your body."

For some reason Zac didn't understand, that made his dick twitch. He pulled on socks and shoes. "I'm ready."

"Not quite. Hands behind your back, Zac."

Marcus approached him, strip of leather in his hand. "This is a play collar. It has no meaning other than as a tool. The only reason I'm telling you that is because for some Doms, a collar has a great deal of significance. Being offered one can be a sign of deep commitment." He fastened the collar around Zac's neck and tested its fit. There was a D-ring at the front and Marcus attached a lead to it. "I want you to concentrate on walking one step behind me. Do you understand?" Zac nodded. He wasn't sure how he felt about being led around like some kind of pet. "Let's go."

It took a lot more focus than Zac expected to avoid bumping into Marcus. He had to anticipate when he was going to slow down or speed up, when he was going to pause. He had to read his body movements, and as they walked it dawned on him why Marcus had done this. They reached the snug where they had eaten the previous evening, and Marcus led him to a chair. He looped the handle of the leash around the chair back then took the other seat.

"I can see you understand."

"As we moved, I wasn't able to think about anything except you. There could be no distractions. I had to anticipate your movements. I think it would take quite a lot of practice to get right."

"For a first attempt, you didn't do badly at all," Marcus said, smiling. "You only bumped into me a couple of times."

"I had to work at getting my headspace away from humiliation and towards pleasing you."

"Not everyone can make that move. For someone who only feels shame or discomfort, it'll never work."

"So it was a test?"

"Of sorts. It tells me that you are able to put aside your pride. That you can put a Dom's needs first and that you recognize that something which might seem simple on the surface is not always so."

The door opened, and Skye arrived pushing a trolley, bright smile in place. "Good afternoon. I have a tureen of Tor's amazing vegetable soup for you and some home-baked bread. There's water or juice then fruit or carrot cake for afters. Luke said I had too much of the cake but I had to test it so I could give you an honest assessment. Both are yummy."

"Thank you for your dedication, Skye," Marcus said. "Everything looks delicious."

The simple praise made Skye glow with happiness. "You're welcome. I'll leave you in peace. I'll refresh your room while you're eating." He bounced out of the snug.

"I think I'm supposed to take care of our room." Zac wondered if he should go after Skye.

"That boy is riding a sugar rush," Marcus said. "Leave him be. Luke will be grateful he's working off some of that energy."

"He comes out of his shell when he gets to know people a little. Luke told me he's usually very shy."

"His master gives him confidence."

"I can quite understand how he'd have that effect. He dotes on Skye."

"You want that? A Dom who adores you?"

"I guess I want that kind of contentment. I think that's something to aspire to in a relationship."

"It's a worthwhile goal but difficult to find." Marcus served soup for both of them using the ladle in the terrine. "Eat as much or as little as you want. We had a decent breakfast so I'm not that hungry, but you've expended more energy than me so far today."

"Thanks." Zac took his first spoonful of soup. "Wow, this is incredible. I am quite hungry."

They ate at an easy pace, Zac opting for some fruit after his soup. He gave the cake a regretful look. "Maybe we could have some of that later, I think I'm full."

"Afternoon tea is a fine tradition." Marcus patted his stomach. "The weather looks good. How about we take a stroll around the grounds?"

"Are you asking me or telling me, Marcus?"

"Don't get cocky, brat. I may be leaving you this evening, but there's still plenty of time to turn your backside red."

"Sorry." Zac had a sudden urge to stay seated so that Marcus couldn't get at his rear.

"I don't think you are." Marcus chuckled. He stood, unlooped Zac's leash from the chair then gave it a tug. "Let's go."

Thinking more about how a spanking might play out, Zac wasn't concentrating and stumbled into Marcus' side. Marcus gave an exaggerated sigh and shook his head. "You definitely need more practice."

Chapter Ten

Dale was thinking about packing away his tools when he spotted Marcus leading Zac into the grounds. He tracked them for a while trying to ignore the uncomfortable knot in his stomach. Marcus had every right to put a collar and leash on Zac, but Dale had to resist the urge to run after them and take possession of the strip of leather. Collars were important, not to be taken lightly. Zac seemed to be doing a decent job of walking at heel, his gaze fixed on Marcus' shoulder. They were talking, and Zac seemed relaxed.

"None of my business," Dale muttered, not for the first time. He put his grumpy reaction down to being tired. He needed to sleep before taking another nightshift but first he had to pack everything away then go and see Luke. He cleaned off the tools he'd used then stowed them in the shed. As he made his way around the building toward the front door, a slight buzzing caught his attention and he swatted at his face in case he was the intended target of a hungry mosquito. Despite his flapping the buzzing continued, getting slightly louder. He looked around for the source of the noise and caught sight of something in the sky above him. Taking care not to make it obvious he'd spotted it, he bent to lace his boot. He fiddled around as long as he dared, watching what he now recognized as a drone out of the corner of his eye. The machine was quite high, and as Dale stood, it flew in the direction Marcus and Zac had walked.

Dale debated whether or not to go after them but decided against it. If he alerted them to the drone, he would also be alerting its operator. Marcus wouldn't take Zac outside the grounds, so he was safe enough for the moment.

Dale went around to the front of the property. He took off his muddy boots, leaving them inside the door before heading for Luke's office. He gave the door a tap and it swung open.

Luke put down his pen. "Come on in, Dale. Would you like a cup of coffee?"

"That would be great, if you have any decaf. I can't believe I'm saying that, but I need to grab a few hours' sleep if I'm going to stay awake again tonight. I need to save the caffeine for later."

Luke pressed some buttons on his desk phone and connected to the kitchen where he ordered coffee from Rayne, who promised to bring it straight away.

"Tor told me you're making great progress on extending the garden, but I guess that's not what you're here to talk about," Luke said.

"And you'd be right. There are a few things I need to tell you. Actually, I was wondering if you'd want Tor to be in on this conversation as well. Sorry, I should have said something before. I'm tired and not thinking straight." Luke picked up the phone again and asked

Rayne to get Tor to bring the coffee because he needed a word. Dale tilted his head from side to side, making his joints crack. "I'm not as used to keeping strange hours as I was."

"But you never quite lose that knack, do you? Like riding a bike."

Dale nodded. "I'll wait until Tor gets here if you don't mind. I don't want to say everything twice."

"Of course. Why don't you sit down?"

"Okay but be warned, there's a chance I might not get up again." Dale sagged into the chair. "I saw Zac outside, with Marcus."

"His time with his first Dom is nearly over. I spoke to Marcus last night, and he was pleased with the way things were going."

"That's…good?"

"I guess it is. Marcus was a nice gentle start for him. His next Dom is very different."

Dale gave a noncommittal grunt and was saved from having to comment further by Tor arriving with coffee. They arranged themselves and their drinks around Luke's desk and once they were all settled, Luke invited Dale to update them.

"Two things, one potentially more worrying than the other. I was out and about last night outside the perimeter wall. I walked the whole distance and I'm glad to say that there are only a limited number of places where access is a possibility. That's the good news. The bad news is that I found a spot where a vehicle had been parked on more than one occasion. It was about as far from the main gates as you can get, near that unmetalled road which meets the B2700. Indents from the tires suggest that it was the same vehicle on different occasions because the positioning moved by a little each time. I'd estimate it had been there three times at least. There were sunflower seed shells in the grass as if someone had spent a deal of time there snacking on them. Now, before you say anything, I realize it could be a regular parking up spot for a local on his lunch break, or there could be some other innocent explanation, but it spiked my interest let's say."

"Unlikely that a local would pick that spot," Tor said. "That's nowhere near civilization."

"I have to agree," Luke said. "There are far better places to pull over. The south side of our perimeter is pretty remote and not an obvious place to go to for a break."

"I didn't see anything else and I've fixed up a few cameras in the area in the hope that we might catch whoever it is on video. I intend to go out early tonight and take another look because not long ago I spotted something more worrying. As I was coming inside from the garden, a drone flew overhead. It happened to be at the time that Marcus and Zac were walking in the grounds. Again, there could be an innocent explanation but somehow, I doubt it. The timing is far too much of a coincidence. I don't like coincidences."

"Me either. A drone? That's not good." Luke sipped his coffee, brow furrowed. "I'll have to let Carey know, and he'll feel obliged to inform Zac's father."

"There's no legitimate reason to be flying a drone over our grounds. What's next, Dale, and how can we help?" Tor asked.

"I took care to give the impression that I hadn't noticed the drone. I'm hoping that the camera operator will note me as the gardener, nothing else. Zac and Marcus were engrossed in conversation, so I doubt they spotted it. It was quite high and it was the buzzing noise it made that attracted my attention. It's unlikely they would have heard it while they were talking." He frowned "I know Marcus is leaving this evening, but I would definitely advise that Zac is never left alone."

"I could suggest that he, Skye and Rayne have a film night after dinner. That should keep the three of them out of trouble," Luke said. "Well, some trouble anyway."

Dale nodded. "Good idea. I'm going to go get some sleep now then head out again tonight. This time I'll go straight to where I think the vehicle was parked and see if anyone shows up."

"Do you want one of us to come with you in case you run into someone?" Tor asked.

"You guys have a business to run. If I do see anyone, I'll take pictures. I've got no intention of engaging with them at the moment and I'll make sure they don't see me. It's not against the law to park a vehicle next to a wall. Unless they caught them in the act of flying the drone, the best the local police could do them for would be littering, though I doubt sunflower seed shells qualify. If they're using a drone, that suggests they're getting the lay of the land. It's unfortunate that Zac happened to be outside at the time, though I imagine they already know he's here."

"They could have tracked him from the States for all we know," Luke said.

"It could still be nothing." Dale hoped it was true, but he didn't believe in coincidences and when it came to Zac's safety he was always going to err on the side of caution. If that made him a suspicious, paranoid, son of a bitch, then so be it.

"Yeah, and Rayne's smart mouth is a passing phase," Tor said.

"Is all not harmonious in the kitchen?" Dale asked, glad for a switch of subject.

"That boy needs taking in hand. He's out of control. Today he made a model of a man with my utensils. He used my favorite hand whisk as his dick."

"We're fortunate he didn't make cookie cocks. You realize that he's been playing up to get your attention," said Luke. "Why don't you bite the bullet, Tor, and do what you've been wanting to do since you met him? Life's short. I wasted a lot of time before I found Skye. It was watching Lorcan and Rowan that convinced me to be less cautious. They were a couple that met here at The Retreat, Dale. We lost an excellent house boy to an American billionaire. A friend of Zac and his father, as it happens."

"You should go for it, Tor," Dale said. "Luke's right and if you don't grasp the nettle, someone else will. Rayne's not malicious and he's pretty. He won't wait forever."

"He's a handful."

"And that suits you down to the ground," Luke observed. "Use the week and a half you have left with him in the kitchen as a trial period."

Dale wished he had the same opportunity with Zac but that was never going to happen. Tor tapped his fingers on his knee. "I suppose he's worth the effort."

"Yes, he is. There's a sweet submissive somewhere underneath all that brat," Luke said, smiling.

"I know. But what if he doesn't want a beat-up ex-soldier who knows how to cook?"

"Beat-up ex-soldiers are a catch," Dale said, quirking his lips.

"He's right. Besides, Rayne's had plenty of time to let you know that he's not interested," Luke added. "Yet he keeps nipping at your ankles."

"I think dealing with a possible kidnap threat would be easier." Tor gave a wry grin.

The three of them drank the rest of their coffee in contemplative silence before Dale made his way back to the garage block. He was flagging and needed to sleep. After a quick shower and a sandwich made from supplies someone had left in the apartment's fridge, he lay in bed staring at the ceiling. It was Tor's hesitance about developing a relationship with Rayne that played on his mind. There were a lot of similarities between him and the recalcitrant chef. Both injured in the line of duty, both enjoying second careers, both Dominants hoping for a compatible partner. An image of Zac's face filled Dale's mind and he fisted the sheets in frustration as his cock stiffened. Zac's mouth would have been far preferable to Dale's hand but for now that would have to do.

* * * *

Zac stood on the steps of The Retreat and watched Marcus drive away with a pang of regret. He'd liked Marcus a lot, and the Dom had given him a gentle introduction to power exchange. At some point, Zac realized that it had been Marcus' actions that had turned him on rather than Marcus himself. There was no spark between them that might have indicated the chance of a longer lasting relationship. They'd parted on good terms, and Zac had promised to look Marcus up if he were ever in London, or visiting The Underground, the latter being something he longed to do. As the car disappeared from view, loneliness enveloped Zac. He'd had Marcus' attention solely on him for the last two days and now he didn't quite know what to do, with no one to give him an order.

Skye appeared on the steps next to him. "How about a mug of cocoa in the staff room?"

"Your timing is perfect. That sounds nice."

Skye slung an arm around Zac's shoulders, and they went inside, traversing the hall and the banqueting room to get to the staff area next to the kitchen. "I bet it feels odd, doesn't it?" Skye asked. "Going from such an intense situation to being left alone."

"Odd's one way of putting it," Zac replied. "I feel a bit lost."

"I understand completely. I feel that way when Luke isn't around. I find myself seeking him out and if he's away from The Retreat completely, I'm never happy."

"I'm not unhappy. I mean, I hardly knew Marcus, though he was super nice. It's going from having someone telling me what to do, directing me, to being left to my own devices again."

"He gave you after-care, though, didn't he?" Skye sounded unusually fierce. "That's so important after a scene. The power of cuddles should not be underestimated."

"He was kind and attentive after each scene, but I didn't get cuddles."

"I'm so sorry!" Skye wrapped him in a hug. "Does this help?"

"It does, thanks, Skye. I'll write cuddles into any future contract as a requirement."

"You so should." They drew apart.

"I don't know why I'm sad. I've no reason to be."

"You need cheering up, which is why you should join Rayne and me for movie night," Skye declared. "There's a big TV in the snug, and we have Netflix, Disney Channel and Amazon Prime. They're all for the guests, of course. But you're a guest, and Rayne and I are your friends, so you can invite us. There must be something we can find that we all enjoy, and I'll tell Rayne he has to be quiet and not give away the plot. I can ask Tor for snacks, and we can have a puppy pile on the floor with cushions and blankets." Skye's enthusiasm was infectious.

"That sounds perfect," Zac said. "Just no French art-house movies, okay?"

"Just because I'm an academic doesn't mean I like all that highbrow stuff," Skye said, giggling. "And Rayne would run away. We've already done James Bond, but I like comedies the most. Rayne likes anything with explosions. I guess we should be able to find a film that has both." He wandered into the kitchen. "There's no one here. You'll have to wait a bit while I heat some milk, okay?" Zac went to join him.

"Where are Tor and Rayne?"

"After we'd finished clearing up from dinner, Tor dragged Rayne off to his room. I'm not sure what he had planned, but Rayne wasn't complaining." Skye put milk in a pan to warm then pulled cocoa and mugs from a cupboard.

"Will he want to join us if he's having fun with Tor?"

"We'd already decided. Rayne won't stand us up and besides, he can have Tor to himself for the rest of the night if he wants to."

"They're finally getting it together then?"

"Looks that way. Tor had a very determined expression at dinner. If I were Rayne I'd have been nervous."

"I'm sorry I missed it. It sounds like it would have been more fun in here with you guys than in the snug with Marcus, though I did need a chance to thank him for all he's done over the last two days. He really opened my eyes to a few things."

"I'll bet." Skye seemed to be fighting to keep a straight face.

"Juvenile."

"Oh, come on, you left yourself wide open there." Skye made their drinks, and they returned to the staff room. They were halfway through their cocoa when Rayne danced into the room. He plopped into a chair, a huge grin across his face. "Hey, guys. What's up?"

"We're plotting our film evening, but more to the point what have you been up to?" Skye waggled his mug in Rayne's direction.

"I've been with Tor. He's evil. Sooo evil." He bent forward and rested his head on his folded arms. "And he has a huge cock."

"Rayne!" Skye exclaimed. "TMI, my friend. Zac is a guest. What will he think of us?"

"I think you're both really lucky," Zac said, chuckling. "Uh, how big exactly?"

Rayne held his hands up a fair width apart, and Zac gaped.

"That's a trout, not a penis," Skye said primly.

Rayne drew his hands together a fraction. "Okay, so maybe I'm over-egging it a bit."

"So the two of you finally..." Skye made a whirling motion with his finger in the air.

"I've no idea what that means," Rayne said, peering up from his arms, "But yeah, we did. We so did. Twice. Took fucking long enough. I've been trying to get in that man's trousers for months."

Skye and Zac exchanged glances then both burst out laughing.

"Shut it, the two of you. I'm giving up an evening of gourmet sex for you pair of reprobates and I'm talking several Michelin stars here." Rayne dragged his fingers through his hair and gave himself a shake. "So, Skye has Luke, I have Tor, all that's left is to fix Zac up with the hot gardener."

Zac scowled. "What are you talking about? Did Tor dissolve your brains?"

"Not entirely. I've seen the way you look at Dale, and he's just as bad. He looks like he wants to pin you to the nearest flat surface, then screw you on it. I'll bet he has a huge…screwdriver." Rayne buffed his nails on his sleeve.

Zac didn't know where to look. "You're imagining things. Marcus only left minutes ago, and after a day off tomorrow I have another Dom arriving, then two more after that."

"Dom, Dom, Dom…" Rayne sang with a dramatic flourish. "I don't know why you're bothering when that superb piece of dominance is wandering around the grounds every day. All that digging sure has given him some muscles too. Yum." He smacked his lips together.

"I think we should go back to discussing films, it's safer," Zac said. He thought Rayne might not give up on the topic, but the redhead just shrugged.

"Anything with explosions is good with me. There's gonna be snacks, right? Coz I need to replenish my energy reserves. Tor drained them, if you know what I mean?"

"Oh my God, Rayne. Stop." Skye gathered up his and Zac's mugs and took them through to the kitchen. "Get in here, you two. If we're going to raid Tor's supplies I need help, and when we get caught, which we will, I'm not taking the fallout alone."

"Mmm, punishment... Has potential," Rayne called. "We're on our way."

Chapter Eleven

Despite a fun evening and a peaceful night's sleep, when Zac awoke the next morning, he didn't quite know what to do with himself. He had fallen into following another man's orders with ease and now he didn't have to do that, he was consumed by uncertainty. Parts of his body ached a little more than they should, a result of the different stresses and strains on his muscles from the previous two days so he decided to go for a swim before hunting down some breakfast. He pulled on some trunks and a pair of loose sweats then shoved his feet into a comfortable pair of Vans before heading downstairs. It was early but he could hear the faint sounds of a radio coming from the direction of the kitchen. Someone — Rayne, he thought — was singing along but the sound faded as he headed to the back of the building where the gym and pool were housed.

The pool wasn't big but had a current to swim against, and Zac felt the need to exercise enough that his mind would have something to contemplate other than what his next Dom might be like. He pushed open the door and found that someone had beaten him to it. Dale was swimming hard, powering up and down the short lengths like a great white was after him. He had a smooth action, cutting through the water with efficient strokes. Zac stood and watched for a while, acknowledging a newly emerging voyeuristic streak. A good five minutes passed before Dale came to a stop at the end of the pool nearest where Zac was standing. He rested his arms on the side and frowned.

"I didn't expect you to be up yet. I'll get out and leave you in peace."

"No! I mean, there's no need. I don't want to interrupt your swim and there's plenty of room for both of us." Zac stripped out of his shoes and bottoms before Dale could object. He took a quick poolside shower then sat on the edge, dangling his legs into the water. It was cool but not cold. Dale turned around and stood with his back resting against the side. His chest was a work of art, glistening with water droplets, the muscles well-defined along with the curve of his biceps. Zac was blessed with a much slighter frame and, though he was trim, he'd never managed the kind of muscle definition that Dale had. *So pretty, I could sit here and watch him all day.*

"Like what you see?" Dale didn't seem upset at the scrutiny.

"Yes." Zac didn't see the point in lying, and it was too early to come up with a smart retort.

Dale grunted. "Are you getting in or are you going to sit there all morning?"

Zac wanted Dale to give him an order. To tell him what to do. He hesitated. "Get in, Zac. Twenty lengths as a warm-up, then I'll put the current machine on for some proper exercise."

Zac slipped into the water and stood letting his body adjust to the temperature. Dale had dealt with his procrastination without fuss. It gave Zac a sense of contentment, of rightness that Dale had given him direction. He began to swim, starting with a leisurely breaststroke before moving on to a faster front crawl. He sensed Dale keeping pace with him but focused on regulating his breathing and keeping his rhythm smooth. Twenty lengths didn't take long in the twenty-five-meter pool, but it was enough effort to speed up his breathing and he was glad to pause in the shallow end for a break.

"You're good," Dale said. "Economical with your movements. You don't waste energy for no reason."

"Lots of practice," Zac said. At the house in Arizona, there was a beautiful pool, and it was no hardship to exercise there every day. He'd managed to keep up the habit at university, finding the quietest sessions to keep his bodyguard happy.

Dale pulled himself from the water then padded along the side to the controls for the tide machine. Zac watched him, reminding himself that his tongue should not be hanging as if he were a happy Labrador. Dale wore a pair of plain black trunks that had no right to be as sexy as they were. He had the kind of body that Zac would have paid good money to explore in detail. Preferably with his tongue.

Once the water began to churn with a current, Dale returned to the pool. Denied the inspiring view of Dale's body, Zac plunged forward and began to swim hard against the flow. There was no longer any room in his head for anything but rapid strokes and deep breaths. It was hard work, and it wasn't long before he began to tire. He pushed himself further but once the burn of lactic acid ignited in his muscles, he moved to the side. Dale was still going, apparently unaffected by the punishing exercise. Zac took a few heaving breaths and admired him, wondering at how fit he must be. After another ten minutes, Dale let the current carry him to the edge. He ducked his head beneath the water then stood, droplets cascading from his shoulders. He rubbed a hand over his head, sluicing the water away.

"You want to join me in the hot tub for a few minutes?" he asked, raising his voice to compete with the sound of the churning water.

Zac nodded. *Dumbest question ever! Try and stop me.* He clambered from the pool with a lot less grace than Dale who went to switch off the tide machine. The hot tub was in the corner of the pool room and Dale made it there first, turning on the bubbles. Zac climbed in then sank beneath the hot water, letting the heat penetrate his muscles.

"This feels great."

"It's a good way to relax after some hard exercise," Dale said. "Are you sure you don't mind me being here?"

"I'm glad you are." Zac worried at his bottom lip little. "Actually, I was going to ask if it would be okay to spend the day with you again."

"You're a glutton for punishment, aren't you?"

Any kind of punishment from you would be fantastic. Zac kept his thoughts to himself. There was no way a Dom like Dale would be interested in an inexperienced sub like him. "I suppose I am." He gave Dale a cheeky grin. "As I've been finding out recently."

Dale rolled his eyes "I won't be towing you around the gardens on a leash."

"You saw that? I wasn't very good at it."

"I caught a glimpse and it looked like you were doing fine to me. Did you enjoy your time with Marcus?"

"He was kind and patient. He taught me a lot in a very short time."

"But?"

"He was maybe a bit too kind." Dale's gaze was piercing, and Zac had to look away. "He gave me too much time to think. I want... I need to be taken to another level."

"You're talking about subspace."

"I've read about it. It feels like a goal that is out of reach for me at the moment. I'm not sure I'm going to be able to let go enough to achieve that kind of state of mind."

"It takes a lot of trust. You need to be with the right man. Some subs slip into it easily, but others take time. It'll happen when the time's right."

"I'm beginning to realize that. I don't know how people do it, going to a club and giving themselves over to another man without a second thought. I don't think that's me. This is much harder than I thought it would be."

"You shouldn't get disheartened. You might feel closer to your next visiting Dom."

I'd rather get closer to you. Zac rested the back of his head on the rim of the tub and closed his eyes. Despite a decent night's sleep, he was weary.

"You can spend the day with me if you really want to. It won't be glamorous."

Zac tried not to betray his delight. He peeked through his lashes at Dale who was massaging his thigh beneath the water.

"Is your leg bothering you?" Zac asked.

"A bit. Running too hard to keep up with Mr. Redding, I'm afraid. He's a natural runner, and I'm sure he was slowing down to accommodate me hence the swim this morning rather than pounding around the perimeter."

"If you like, I could give you a massage. I'm quite good at it. My dad tore ligaments in his shoulder a few years ago and still gets problems, so I learned how to do it. He never had time to get to an appointment and didn't like inviting strangers to the house." *And I'd really like to get my hands on your bare skin.*

"We'll see. We have a day in the garden to get through and that'll loosen me up some." Dale rose, and Zac found himself face-to-groin. The bulge in Dale's swimming trunks was intimidating to say the least. Zac had to resist the urge to lean forward and nuzzle the wet fabric. He made eye contact with Dale and knew there and then that the positioning was deliberate. Dale's dark eyes glinted, and he smirked. "Time to go. You can join me for breakfast in the staff dining room." He turned to climb out of the tub, and Zac's breath hitched as he exchanged his view of Dale's crotch for one of his backside.

"Wowsers." He hoped the churning water had masked the sound of his voice because he hadn't meant to say that out loud.

"Are you coming?"

"No, but I'm not far off," he muttered. "Right behind you!" He wasn't sure how he was going to survive in the shower room if Dale stripped off in front of him.

Zac's dick was already trying to escape his swim shorts. He scrambled from the tub to follow Dale down the side of the pool toward the changing room, feet slapping on the tiles. He grabbed his shoes and sweats, holding them away from his wet body as he went into the showers. He left his stuff on a bench then rounded the lockers to the communal shower area. There were no cubicles but walls to waist height gave some privacy and Dale was already showering, lathering his body with gel from a wall dispenser. The scent of lemons filled the air. Just like everything else at The Retreat, the toiletries were high-end and the black, fluffy towels luxurious. Zac couldn't have cared less if he'd had to use dish soap and a towel harder than sandpaper. Occupying the stall next to Dale was the stuff dreams were made of. Getting the chlorine off his skin was the last thing on his mind as he dropped his swim shorts. He pumped out some gel then grabbed his cock.

"Touch that and you'll be clearing brambles for the rest of the day," Dale snapped.

"You can't..." Zac moved his hand away from his aching shaft.

"Can't what?"

"Nothing, Sir." Zac rested his head against the cool tile in front of him and ignored Dale's low chuckle.

"If you're good, I might decide to let you come later."

"Is that usually part of gardening?"

"It is if you're doing it with me. I think we've moved past the garden lackey stage, don't you?" Butt naked, Dale strolled past Zac's stall. Against his better judgment, Zac turned at the last minute and caught sight of Dale's glorious ass as he rounded the lockers. He whimpered.

"Why did you look, you idiot?" His dick was rock-hard and aching. He rinsed then did the only thing he could think of—he turned the water to cold. "Holy fucking Christ!" The shock did its job, wilting his erection but it left him shivering. He grabbed a towel and wrapped himself up like a mummy, teeth chattering. He went to retrieve his sweats and found Dale already dressed.

"You're a little blue-tinged."

"Wakes me up if the last blast of water is cold," Zac lied.

"Really. Nothing to do with that pretty cock of yours then? Get warm. I'll see you in the dining room."

He was looking at my dick! Zac wasn't imagining the challenge in Dale's eyes. He nodded. "I'll be there."

"Wear old gear. I have a suspicion you'll be getting dirty today."

Zac was certain Dale wasn't talking about common or garden mud. "That's not fair!" He was talking to himself because Dale had already gone. Zac gave his rising cock a baleful glare. "I am *not* taking another cold shower." He finished drying, pulled on his sweats then jogged back to his room to find old clothes. Not that anyone would have batted an eyelid if he'd run around the place naked. By the time he got to the staff dining room, breakfast was in full swing. He slipped into the free seat next to Dale.

"For a fee-paying guest, you sure like to rough it," Rayne said as he chomped on a sausage.

"Tor's food is great wherever it gets eaten," Zac said, sending Tor a grin.

"Suck up!" Rayne muttered, getting a clip around the ear for this cheek.

"He's a gardener's assistant for the day, so please feed him," Dale said. "He's going to need his energy." He stabbed a hash brown in the dish in the center of the table then transferred it to his plate.

"I'll have toast and coffee, please," Zac said. "I don't want to create extra work for anyone."

"He'll have a full breakfast, toast, orange juice and coffee," Dale ordered.

"You heard him." Tor flicked Rayne's ear. "Move it, before I motivate you by applying my hand to your behind."

"Oh, I don't want Rayne's food to go cold…"

"It won't. The plates are hot, and it won't take him a minute to refresh the dishes, there's plenty of food staying warm in the oven."

To Zac's surprise, Rayne planted a smacking kiss right on Tor's lips before leaving his seat. Luke, who was reading the paper, glasses perched on the end of his nose, smirked.

"Awww!" Skye leaned against Luke. "Aren't they cute?"

"Very cute, sweetheart."

Tor scowled. "I am not cute! If there wasn't a guest present…"

"Don't mind me." Zac laughed. "This is fun!"

"Deal with him, Dale," Tor growled. "Rayne's a bad influence on him."

"What about me?" Skye piped up. "I want to be a bad influence too."

"I think you need a bit more practice, love. Besides, I'd prefer you stay as sweet as you are." Luke ruffled Skye's hair, before giving him a lingering kiss.

Rayne returned with fresh toast and coffee, and Zac helped himself from the dishes in the center of the table.

He heaped his plate until Dale gave a grunt of satisfaction.

"Eat. Behave yourself and you might get through the day without a spanking."

Zac caught the glance that Tor and Luke shared and the knowing expressions that followed. He wondered if there was some kind of secret Dom code that he didn't know about because they were definitely communicating. He caught Skye's eye and got a reassuring smile.

"Food's good, isn't it?" Skye helped himself to more scrambled eggs. "Tor is a kitchen magician."

Grateful for a safe topic, Zac nodded. "Best food I've ever tasted. I was hungrier than I thought. That seems to be a recurring theme around here. I think I have no appetite but then I taste Tor's cooking."

"Working in the garden is hard. I'd rather be pushing the vacuum around the house than manhandling a wheelbarrow."

"And you have plenty of hoovering to do, so unless you want to be doing housework naked, finish your breakfast." Luke didn't even look up from his paper. Skye's eyes widened and he crunched down his last corner of toast. Zac wouldn't be surprised at all if Luke followed through on that threat. *Or is it a promise?* He hoped Dale didn't consider naked gardening a good thing. There were a lot of possibilities for uncomfortable bites, stings and scratches.

"At least there aren't any snakes here," Zac said. Several sets of eyes turned his way.

"Where did that come from?" Rayne asked.

"I was just thinking that Arizona has fifty-two species of snake. Thirteen of them are types of rattler. It makes yard work a whole different concept."

"Fifty-two!" Skye paled. "That's an awful lot of nope ropes."

"I prefer danger noodles," Rayne said.

"You two both spend too much time on social media," Luke commented.

"Don't worry, I won't be asking you to work naked," Dale said, face expressionless.

"How did you—? Never mind." Zac swallowed more coffee, ignoring Skye and Rayne's obvious amusement.

"Ready?" Dale pushed his chair back. "Thank you for breakfast, Tor."

Zac got to his feet, wondering at his life choices. Dale might turn out to be more than he could handle.

Chapter Twelve

Dale dumped a final barrow load of topsoil in one of the new raised beds then stretched, easing his aching back. Not far away, under the shade of a towering oak, Zac had flopped in the grass. He was shading his eyes with one arm as sunlight flickered through the leaves, casting dappled patterns across his body. He was smiling and there was a smear of dirt across one cheek. Dale smiled too until he noted a long scratch that ran the length of Zac's forearm.

"I think you killed me," Zac murmured, moving his arm, blinking in the brightness.

"You're still breathing. A decent day's work won't do you any harm." Dale sat on the grass next to him. He winced, as his hip twinged. "Don't say a word."

"I wouldn't dare."

"You're thinking it, though, aren't you?"

"No. Not a thought in my head."

"I don't believe that for a second. Once we've cleared up, we need to get that scratch on your arm seen to. It looks quite nasty. I think I spotted a first-aid kit back at my apartment."

Zac examined his arm as if he'd not noticed the injury before. "That bramble patch got its revenge." He prodded at the wound. "It doesn't hurt much. It's not that deep." The cut oozed a few drops of blood where he'd worried at it.

"Stop that." Dale pushed Zac's hand away. "If you get an infection from a dirty cut, you won't be any use to me."

"Sweet of you to care."

"Sweet? That could be further from the truth, and besides, Luke would kill me if you got too damaged."

"I think you like to come across as a big, bad Dom but underneath you're all soft and squishy."

"I should spank you just for thinking something like that, let alone saying it."

"You probably should."

"You have another Dom arriving tomorrow, don't you? Perhaps I'll leave him a note telling him to give you a good paddling."

"That's... You wouldn't?" Zac didn't sound convinced.

"Wouldn't I? Are you sure about that?"

Dale held out a hand, which Zac took. He hauled Zac to his feet, holding on a fraction longer than necessary. To Dale's satisfaction, Zac made no attempt to pull away. On the contrary, he seemed disappointed when Dale released his hand. The temptation to drag Zac somewhere quiet and fuck him hard was strong especially as Dale got the feeling Zac wouldn't object.

It's not the time and not my place. Pull yourself together, you fucking idiot. "We'll put the tools away then I'll see to your arm. I wasn't joking about that. At the very least it needs cleaning with some antiseptic. Are you up to date with your tetanus vaccinations?"

"Yeah, Dad always made sure I got all the shots going—especially if we were visiting more remote places. He's very fond of parts of Africa and Latin America. Beautiful, but loads of bitey things wandering around the place. I found a scorpion in one of my walking boots once."

"That sounds...unnerving. If you're jabbed, some basic first aid should cover it, though I may now get creepy-crawly-related nightmares tonight so thanks for that." Dale piled the smaller tools into the barrow. Zac picked up the two larger spades they'd been using then they strolled across to the shed. Zac went inside and as he did, Dale heard a familiar whining sound. He dropped the barrow handles then turned to see a drone heading straight for him, at head height. The machine was weaving and bucking as if out of control. Dale had a split second to react and slewed violently to one side. The drone caught his shoulder, then did a crazy spin into the nearest tree before crashing to the ground where it lay hidden in the undergrowth.

"Fuck!" Dale rubbed at his shoulder. "That's gonna bruise."

"Sorry, what?" Zac emerged from the dim depths of the shed.

"Nothing. I was talking to myself. Banged my thigh on the wheelbarrow."

"Oh. Okay. Are you all right?"

"Sure, just annoyed with myself. It's nothing." Dale handed tools across to Zac, who put them away. Once that was done, Dale wheeled the barrow to one side, tilting it against the shed wall so it wouldn't gather water in case of rain. He padlocked the shed then led the way back toward the garage block.

"The apartment's not locked. Why don't you go ahead while I let Luke know that you're with me? I don't want him worrying that you've gone AWOL."

"Sure. Is it okay if I use your shower?" Zac asked. "I stink."

Dale didn't object to the scent of hard work, but he nodded. "Sure. Help yourself, I won't be long. There are plenty of towels in the closet, and you can use my toiletries." Once Zac had rounded the corner of the building, Dale went inside, after toeing off his boots, to find Luke. He was in his office working and he was alone.

"Dale, have you finished in the garden for the day? You've had decent weather for it."

Dale nodded. "I got a lot done with Zac's help, but the drone appeared again. I think it had some kind of mechanical failure because it crashed into the trees near the shed after nearly taking my head off. Zac was stowing tools away in the shed at the time, so he didn't see it and it wasn't visible where it landed. I sent him back to my apartment because he has a nasty scratch that I want to take care of. Could you or Tor go and retrieve the drone without anyone else noticing?"

"Of course. Skye's using the pool at the moment, so I'll be able to get it. Tor and Rayne are in the kitchen. You're not hurt?"

"It was a glancing blow, nothing serious. If I hadn't seen it coming it could have been a lot worse. I thought about going outside to see if the operator was still there, but I had Zac with me."

"I'll go take a look myself," Luke said, his expression stone cold. "Whoever it was is probably long gone, though. They could have killed you."

"I'll take a look round in the early hours but I don't intend to spend the whole night on watch again. Whoever this was won't be stupid enough to come back again anytime soon."

"Let's talk after dinner. We can look over the drone while we keep the boys occupied somewhere else. Once I've picked it up, I'll store it here in the office. No one but Skye comes in here if I'm not working but he should be occupied elsewhere."

Dale nodded. "Sounds good. I'd best go check on Zac."

"I think that would be wise."

"What?" Dale caught something in Luke's expression.

"Nothing. We'll talk later."

Dale scowled at Luke's smirk. "Why do I get the feeling there's something going on around here that I'm not privy to?"

"Suspicious mind?"

"Definitely. Going now." Dale retrieved his boots then marched from Luke's office around the building to the garage block. The first thing he heard when he got inside the apartment was the sound of running water and his mind instantly filled with images of a naked Zac in the shower. *God help me.* His cock hardened faster than was comfortable. He unlaced his boots again, leaving them near the door then padded to the bathroom. The door was ajar, the room filled with steam. Dale leaned against the wall next to the door, facing away so that he wasn't tempted to take a peek.

"You okay in there? Did you find everything you need?"

"Dale, I'm glad you're here. I forgot about a towel. Could you hand me one? I'm about done."

Dale pressed the heel of his hand to his erection, willing it to go down. "I'll fetch one. Stay put a second." He had to walk the length of the apartment to the bedroom closet to get a fresh towel. The distance wasn't nearly far enough. A ten mile yomp through the forest wouldn't be enough to do anything about his physical predicament while Zac was in his shower.

A pair of bright green eye met his as he entered the bedroom. A cat, a big, fluffy cat, was stretched out on the bed. "How did you get in here?" Dale went over to the bed, reaching out a hand for the cat to sniff. "I suppose Zac encouraged you? Are you Marshmallow or Lucky?" The cat rubbed its head again Dale's fingers. "Whichever, you can't stay in here getting everything hairy." Dale made kissy noises in the hope the fur ball would follow him, but she made no attempt to move. He sighed. "Five minutes while I deliver a towel. Then you're gone."

Stealing himself, Dale leaned into the bathroom. Zac stepped out of the shower cubicle, wet skin gleaming, and Dale forced his line of sight to remain above waist level as he handed over the towel. "Did you have anything to do with the purring thing on my bed?"

"That's Marshmallow. She—actually I don't know whether she's a she or a he—followed me when I came in. She made straight for the bedroom, so I guessed she'd been in before. Don't you like cats?"

"They're cute enough, but I prefer dogs. They respond to commands better."

"Big surprise. Did you evict her?"

"She wasn't in a cooperative mood."

Zac laughed. "Definitely female." The scratch on Zac's arm was bleeding again, and he took his time dabbing at it with a tissue before wrapping the towel around his waist. "Are you going to play doctor now?"

Dale unclenched his gritted teeth. "Role-play isn't my thing." The first-aid kit was in the cupboard under the sink. He balanced it on the vanity unit then pulled out antiseptic cream. "Arm." He smeared cream along the scratch. "I don't think this needs a bandage or anything, but you must keep it clean."

"Thanks. I didn't really think this through," Zac said. "I don't have any clean clothes to put on."

I'd be quite happy if you stayed in that towel. "You can borrow something of mine until you go back to your room." Dale fetched clothes for himself and a clean pair of jogging bottoms and a T-shirt for Zac. When he handed them over, Zac dropped the towel with a smirk before dressing.

"You're treading on very dangerous ground, brat."

"I do hope so," Zac murmured.

"Go make us a pot of coffee while I take a shower," Dale ordered.

"I could scrub your back..."

"Zac... I swear, if you didn't have a new Dom visiting you tomorrow you'd be over my knee faster than could say 'Yanks get spanks'. I don't think whoever it is will appreciate you starting out with a glowing behind however, and that's the only reason I'm letting you off the hook. While I'm in here, you also get to persuade Marshmallow to vacate the premises."

Dale stalked into the bathroom, shutting the door with a click. He'd brought fresh clothes with him so that there was no danger of him having to wander around in a towel. He was in enough trouble as it was. He took advantage of alone time in the shower to jack off, giving himself some much-needed relief. Zac was pushing for something Dale wanted to give but he couldn't let himself be drawn in by those pretty, appealing eyes. Zac's father had paid a no-doubt-obscene amount of money so that his son could experience the best kind of introduction to the world of dominance and submission. He wouldn't be best pleased if those carefully constructed plans were thrown into disarray by the hired help.

I've known him for all of four days. This is lust, pure and simple. Too long without a warm submissive in my bed. It's playing with my sanity.

Zac was in the kitchen making coffee when Dale got there. "It's only instant, I'm afraid."

"It's hot and wet, it'll do."

"Good to know your standards, Dale." Zac grinned.

Dale shook his head. "So help me... Is the cat gone?"

"I had to bribe her with a tin of tuna I found in the cupboard. She followed me outside no problem."

"Bribery... good plan."

"How's your hip? I meant what I said about giving you a massage if you want one."

It was sore. So was Dale's shoulder where the drone had hit him. He'd be a mess of bruising by morning. "It's fine, I've had worse."

"Can you stop being such a hero and let me help you? You're clearly in pain. You probably thought getting shot was a minor inconvenience."

"I was unconscious. I didn't get a say."

"Sorry, I didn't mean to open old wounds so to speak."

"You didn't. It was a long time ago."

"Still…let me make it up to you by easing a few knots."

"You're not going to stop pestering me unless I give in, are you?"

"No, and I can be a thorn in your butt no trouble at all." Zac folded his arms, a picture of obstinacy.

"I think the saying is thorn in the side."

"I'm aiming for somewhere more uncomfortable. You won't be able to sit down because of my thorniness."

"That I don't doubt. Fine. Where do you want me?"

"That's a leading question!"

"Zac, I'm already itching to ask Luke if I can borrow a cane. You have thirty seconds to focus, or things are not going to go well for your behind, visiting Dom or not."

"I… Never mind. Strip off then get on the bed, please. Do you have any oil or lotion or anything?"

"I have heavy duty gardener's hand cream. Will that do?"

"Sure. It might be a bit thick but I can make it work. Best put a towel on the bed so the covers don't get greasy."

Dale muttered curses under his breath as he stripped. He lay on his front and buried his face in his arms. He didn't need to see Zac's expression.

"Your ass is a thing of beauty." The bed bounced as Zac straddled Dale's body.

"Thank you for the unsolicited appraisal. Wait, are you naked?"

"Maybe?"

"Oh God. I need a fucking safe word."

"I didn't want to get anything sticky on my clothes — well, they're your clothes, but you know what I mean."

Dale debated putting a stop to this before it went too far but then Zac dug his fingers into Dale's hip, and he put aside any doubts. The muscles were tight and at first the massage was painful but gradually his body relaxed, and the tension dissolved beneath Zac's clever probing.

"There's so many knots in here I'm surprised you could walk," Zac said. "You also have a mega bruise forming on your shoulder. How did you get that?"

Dale gave a noncommittal grunt. "Must have walked into something. Didn't notice."

"You must have a seriously high pain threshold."

"Much higher than my tolerance for bratty submissives who talk too much."

In response, Zac dug his thumbs into Dale's glutes.

"Holy fucking Christ, that hurts! And you're supposed to be concentrating on my hip, not my ass."

"It's hard to resist when I'm staring straight at it," Zac said. "But seriously, pain in your hip is likely linked to tension here, in your lower back and potentially in other muscles as well. You probably compensate unconsciously for the pain and put additional strain on other areas, so bite on that pillow because I'm not stopping."

"I'll give you bite the fucking pillow," Dale grumbled. He endured Zac's attentions by imagining how he might get his revenge. It involved a bit gag and some cunning predicament bondage. Despite his misgivings, he had to admit that Zac had magic fingers and knew what he was doing. Dale's aches and pains were reducing with every stroke and probe. Zac moved to his lower back then his shoulders, and Dale began to doze while Zac worked steadily, saying nothing for a long while.

"Turn over," Zac eventually said.

"Not a fucking chance," Dale mumbled into his pillow. "How much of an idiot do you think I am?"

"I'd be more than happy to give you a different kind of relief."

Tempting, so tempting. "That was great, Zac, but all that's going to happen now is that you're going to put some clothes on, and I'm going to escort you back to the main building where you're going to spend your evening playing tiddlywinks or watching rubbish on TV because you need to be well rested for tomorrow. Your visiting Dom deserves your respect and attention."

"Can I at least do this again sometime?"

"I'm not sure that's a good idea."

"It's a brilliant idea, and you didn't say no." Zac clambered off the bed, and Dale listened to the rustle of clothing as he dressed. Dale rolled over, taking the towel he was lying on with him so that he was covered.

"Spoilsport." Zac pouted, and Dale wanted to punish that plump lower lip with his teeth.

"I can always leave a few suggestions for your visiting Dom," Dale said, grabbing his clothes. "A nice fat ball gag. Chastity. Hot wax."

Zac's eyes widened. "That's not supposed to be turning me on, is it?"

Dale pulled up his trousers with some relief. His skin was a little oily from the massage, but he'd delay showering again until Zac was a safe distance away and there were several closed doors between them. He slipped his feet into a pair of running shoes. "Let's go. I imagine Tor will be wanting to serve you something amazing for dinner and it wouldn't be polite to keep him waiting." He led Zac across the courtyard and in through the main door of The Retreat where they found Skye dusting furniture.

"Zac! I hope Dale didn't work you too hard today. Are you hungry? It's nearly time for dinner. Tor wanted me to ask where you want to eat."

"Do you think you and Rayne would be allowed to join me in my room?" Zac asked.

"I don't see why not. You're the guest so you get to decide."

"I don't want to put anyone out," Zac said.

"How about I go check with Tor. I think Luke's in the kitchen discussing supplies or something with him."

"Okay, I need to go change anyway. Thanks for today, Dale. It was…inspiring."

Dale growled under his breath. "Skye, could you let Luke know I'd like a word?"

"Sure. He's likely on his way back to his office by now. I'll go intercept him."

Dale paced the length of the hall, but it wasn't long before Luke appeared and gestured for him to come into his office.

"I found it," he said immediately. "It inconveniently crashed in some stinging nettles, and I'd forgotten how much multiple stings can hurt. I got through a lot of dock leaves. I also drove round to the spot where you found signs of someone parking but there was no one there. Not surprising. But the ground was freshly churned so I think that's where they launched the drone from. They may have gotten away but they're down one expensive piece of tech, which is something to celebrate." Luke circled his desk. He pushed his chair back to reveal the drone occupying the seat. "I didn't want to leave it in view in case Skye decided to come in here to clean something. Do you know much about these things?"

"A bit," Dale said. "We used them sometimes in my unit. They don't have the longest battery life. An average drone will fly for about ten minutes, while high-end models will allow you to fly for around twenty to twenty-five minutes, I think. This one looks mid-range to me, a bit more than a starter model that's for sure."

"There's a camera mounted on it," Luke said.

"That's good, we should be able to retrieve the SD card. Drone shots take up a lot of memory space — a two-minute video takes up around a gig, I believe."

"I wonder if it was taking still images or video footage."

"From what I understand, if you are taking still images, you have to fly your drone more slowly. The key is that you want it to remain motionless. Even with a gimbal, which is a balancing mechanism, your shots will become very blurry as you accelerate."

"So you get the sharpest photos when the drone hovers in mid-air?"

"That's right and both times I saw it, it was moving quite fast so I'm guessing that whatever footage it has — stills or video — isn't great quality."

Luke frowned. "Suggests an amateur, which is odd. I did a little bit of web research around the law regarding drone usage too. It varies a lot, but in this country you can't fly within fifty meters of people or property that are not under the direct control of the drone user and you have to ensure any images you obtain using the drone don't break privacy laws." He picked the drone up. "If you're using a drone weighing more than two hundred and fifty grams and need to fly closer than one hundred and fifty meters from a built-up area, you need something called an A2 Certificate of Competency…there's more but basically there are a lot of rules and regulations that have to be adhered to. I suppose it's possible that this guy might be registered, but I don't like our chances."

While Luke held the machine, Dale extracted the SD card from the mounted camera. "Whoever this was, he certainly wasn't bothered about privacy."

"Let me put that into the computer," Luke said, putting the drone on his desk.

Dale handed it over, and Luke pressed it into the slot in the front of his laptop.

When he opened the file it proved to contain grainy video footage, mainly of the grounds. At one point, two blurred figures could be seen walking along the drive.

"That's from when I first saw it," Dale pointed out. "So it looks like everything is on the same card. That's good for us — not that this footage is usable for very much anyway. You certainly can't tell what's going on between Marcus and Zac, and they aren't identifiable."

"I guess the operator could have been viewing the footage on their phone or a screen."

"That's possible, but it wouldn't have been recorded anywhere else."

"There's a serial number on what's left of the drone, I'll get a contact to check out whether it's registered to anyone but I don't hold out much hope. I'll update Carey as well. I spoke to him earlier, and he was going to call Zac's father once time zones allowed. He may know if there have been any recent threats we should be aware of."

"Fair enough," Dale said. "I think it's safe for me to take tonight off. I'll catch up on my rest and be ready to get back out there tomorrow night in case whoever this is comes back."

"Okay. I understand the boys have plans to eat in Zac's room. Would you like to join Tor and me for some dinner?"

"That sounds good. I'm not going to turn down more of Tor's cooking."

"And it'll give us the chance to talk about how you're getting on with young Zac."

"I think that's a topic of conversation we should avoid," Dale said.

"That's telling."

"I swear, Luke, he has some kind of magnetic field drawing me in. It's getting harder and harder to pull away."

"Why not just let it happen?"

"You know why not. He's not for me."

"And what does he have to say about that?"

"That's a question that is far too dangerous to ask."

Chapter Thirteen

Zac sucked on a sticky finger, savoring the last of the sauce that had dripped from his fajita. Tor had produced another feast, and he, Rayne and Skye had had great fun choosing their fillings. They'd demolished the spicy chicken wraps and were now tucking into an enormous bowl of strawberries, all three of them sitting cross-legged on Zac's bed.

"Save some of those berries for me, Skye." Zac dipped into the bowl and picked a juicy red fruit.

"You snooze, you lose. These are my favorites."

Rayne laughed. "It's the only time he gets feral. He's usually so sweet and innocent but present him with a bowl of strawberries and he gets more possessive than Luke."

"I've noticed!" Zac made a grab for the bowl. "It's like he has a second personality."

"The only thing that would make these better," Skye said, ignoring them both, "is a chocolate fondue to dip them in."

"Dad had a chocolate fountain at a dinner party he threw once," Zac said. "I gorged myself. I told myself it was fruit and therefore good for me."

"Kids are allowed to overindulge in chocolate fountains," Skye said. "It's the law."

"I was twenty and home from college for the vacation," Zac admitted, smiling.

"Still justified. Chocolate and fruit go together like subs and Doms."

"Talking of…" Rayne butted in. "How was your day with the hotty gardener?"

"Hard work. That man sure does take pleasure in bossing me around."

"Which you don't enjoy it all." Grinning, Rayne chomped on another strawberry.

"Let's say the day had its moments."

"You wouldn't be hiding something from us, would you Zac?" Rayne narrowed his eyes. "I smell a story and the subs' code means you have to tell."

Mouth full, Skye nodded his agreement.

Zac sighed. "I can't even look at him without getting turned on. What's wrong with me? He says 'put some effort into that digging, Zac', and my dick thinks it's Christmas. And that's when he's fully dressed."

"So you've seen him when he isn't?" Skye and Rayne both leaned closer.

"We were in the swimming pool at the same time this morning," Zac admitted.

"You lucky sod," Rayne said. "Is he as hot as I think he is?"

"He has muscles and tattoos," Zac said dreamily.

"But what about the good stuff? You know, did he fill out his speedos?"

"Rayne, we were in the pool. I wasn't looking at his crotch, I was swimming."

"Uh huh and when he got out of the pool and in the shower?" Rayne prodded Zac's thigh. "You can't tell me you didn't take peek."

"Is it getting hot in here?" Zac fanned his face. "Perhaps I should open the window."

"You did see something!" Skye exclaimed.

"Hard not to in a communal shower," Zac muttered.

"This gets better and better," Rayne crowed. He held up his hands about two feet apart. "I'm guessing this big."

"That's... That's not anatomically possible and besides, I didn't see his front. Tor's filled your mind with size issues."

"So you got to see his butt?"

The image filled Zac's head. "It was a thing of beauty."

"More to the point, he got to see yours," Skye said, blushing.

"He's not interested," Zac said. "I all but begged to blow him, and he didn't take me up on the offer."

"Wait...you what?"

Zac rubbed the heels of his hands into his eye sockets. "After we finished work, we went back to where he's staying because I'd scratched my arm, and he offered to treat it. Actually, that's not true, he didn't offer, he ordered me to go with him."

"Cool!" Skye said.

"Hot, you mean." Rayne nudged Skye. "Carry on, Zac."

"I used his shower, and he loaned me some clothes. His hip was bothering him, so I offered to give him a massage."

"And he accepted?" Skye's eyes were wide.

"Well, I kind of wore him down by nagging him incessantly."

"Can you actually do massage, or were you making it up?" Rayne asked. "Because I would so do that."

"Actually, I can. I did a course so I could help my dad out with a shoulder problem and found I enjoyed it."

"So you got your oily hands all over Dale's yummy body?" Skye was wriggling in place he was so excited.

"Well, not all over him. Just his back."

"But he was naked, right?"

"He was and uh... So was I." Zac blinked. "I was being practical. Massage can get messy, okay?"

"I'll bet it can." Rayne fell about laughing.

"So there we are, we're both naked, oily, on the bed and I'm still a virgin. Says it all, doesn't it?"

"He must have cast-iron willpower, that's all I can say." Rayne gave Zac a sympathetic smile. "So what are you going to do next? You have another Dom arriving tomorrow."

"I don't know. I need advice. There's something about Dale that's hard to ignore. I mean he's gorgeous and all but it's not only that. It's this aura he has. Controlled power. He's so sure of himself but he's not aggressive. I want to do what he tells me. I want to make him happy." He shook his head. "It's so confusing."

Skye patted his arm. "Well, you came here to find out what you're into and it looks like you have. You shouldn't ignore instant attraction. I knew straightaway that I wanted Luke. It happens. And from the sound of it, it's not insta lust, it's more than that. You know we can make whatever arrangements you want regarding the other Doms. Nobody will get upset if you want to change the plan."

"I kinda feel like I should go through with it. The whole idea is to meet different kinds of men in a safe space. I didn't expect to meet one of them in the grounds is all. I don't think it would be fair to cancel everything, especially when Dale is blowing hot and cold."

"Or not blowing at all!" Rayne cackled. "It's horses for courses," Rayne said. "Tor and I have been dancing around each other for ages but the spark was always there. I know I irritate the hell out of him, and he's way too fond of spanking my behind, but we got there. It's different for everyone. I count myself lucky, some men go their entire lifetime without finding that one person that fits them."

"Rayne is right," Skye said. "You mustn't ignore this or let Dale slip through your fingers."

"But how do I convince him that I'm worth his time?" Zac pummeled a pillow before sitting back against the end of the bed. "As far as he's concerned I'm some spoiled, rich kid playing at the edges of a lifestyle he's committed to."

"You're not spoiled." Skye wriggled back so that he was sitting next to Zac. He leaned against him. "We wouldn't be friends if you were. We are friends, aren't we?" He nibbled on his lip.

"Of course we are. I've got closer to you two guys in a few short days than I have with anyone else. Sure, I had buddies at school but when you're walking around with a bodyguard in tow, friendships are hard to maintain."

"It must have been lonely." Skye's brow was furrowed. "It's good you have us now. We need to come up with a plan."

"That sounds like something I can get involved with," Rayne said rubbing his hands together. "Mayhem is my middle name."

"Between the three of us we should be able to cook up with something," Zac said. "Let's hope it doesn't get us into the kind of trouble we can't deal with."

Dale ate the last mouthful of the tenderest lamb he'd ever tasted. He moaned his satisfaction before putting his cutlery on his plate. "That was amazing, Tor. It's going to be really hard to leave this place at the end of my two weeks because I'm going to miss your cooking so much."

Tor raised his glass of wine in a toast. "Your feedback is appreciated, but is that the only thing you're going to miss?"

"I have no idea what you're talking about. Did I hear you say something about jam roly-poly for pudding?"

Tor shook his head. "Give him another drink, Luke. We need to loosen his tongue."

Luke topped up Dale's glass. "I think you deserve this after the effort you've put in over the last few days."

"It'll have to be the last, though—hard labor with a hangover is no fun at all, and I don't have the same capacity for alcohol I did when I was in the army."

"And you won't have your willing assistant with you tomorrow to do the hard labor."

Dale looked from Tor to Luke, both of them wearing speculative expressions. "You're going to withhold my pudding unless I talk, aren't you?"

Tor nodded. "I made my own custard from scratch, too. I use vanilla pods…"

"Sadists, the pair of you. I hope you don't expect me to sit here and talk about my feelings?"

"God forbid." Luke's eyes twinkled.

"I wonder what the boys are talking about."

Dale was grateful for Tor's change of topic.

"It's best not to go there," Luke said. "You really don't want to know. Many a good Dom has asked that question and ended up traumatized."

"Point taken." Tor got up and returned two minutes later with the promised pudding and a jug of steaming custard. "You're not off the hook," Tor said, waving a serving spoon at Dale.

"I respond better to bribery than threats, especially when that bribery is pudding. I don't remember the last time I had jam roly-poly. Probably at primary school where it would have had the consistency of a tire."

"If you compare my version to anything you had at school, I'll take you down to the dungeon and give you a good flogging," Tor said as he doled out sizeable portions before dousing them in custard.

"I wouldn't dream of it. God, do you remember frog spawn tapioca? That stuff was rank."

"I rebelled after a particularly heinous bowl of spotted dick," Tor said. "Started to take in my own packed lunch. That's what sparked my interest in cooking I think because my Mum was happy to give me free rein in the kitchen. She hated cooking."

After a suitable interval for plenty of happy munching, Dale sat back in his seat. "There's no way I can fit in another helping, so I guess I'd better bite the bullet. What do you want to know?"

"You had Zac's company for the entire day again and took him back to your apartment," Luke said. He didn't sound accusatory, just curious. "You like him."

"Whether I do or not is irrelevant," Dale said, wishing it weren't true. "The only reason I took him back to the apartment was to treat a nasty scratch he got from bramble wrangling."

"You know there's a proper first-aid kit in the house and both Tor and I are trained in dealing with minor injuries," Luke said.

Dale shrugged. "We were already together, both filthy from the garden, it made sense to take him back to my place."

"And nothing to do with how protective you're feeling," Tor said.

"Okay, I admit, I like him. He's a natural submissive but there's a spark there. He's not passive, he likes to push."

"Likes to push you, more specifically," Tor mused.

"I'm sure Marcus and the other Doms he's seeing will get the best out of him."

"You don't sound so happy about that." Luke lifted his glass but didn't drink, just swirled the liquid around.

"It's not for me to be happy or unhappy about it, though, is it, Luke? I'm here to look out for him, make sure no harm comes to him."

"Potential harm can come from a range of directions though, can't it?" Luke eyed his empty dish. "That was great, Tor, thank you. I have to resist a second helping too."

"What do you mean? And I'm not talking about seconds," Dale asked.

"I had an interesting conversation with Marcus before he left," Luke said. "He said that Zac is a wonderful young man, very respectful and destined to be an excellent submissive for someone. However, he felt at times that his mind was in another place, like he was thinking too much. Marcus was careful, he gave him quite a gentle introduction to aspects of the lifestyle. The Dom visiting tomorrow is very different. It won't serve Zac well to be thinking about another man while he's playing with Eric."

"Eric Walcott?" Dale asked. "He has a hard-core reputation. Good man, though."

"Yes, you may have come across him at The Underground."

"I did, doing a knife play demonstration. He won't be doing that with Zac, though, surely?"

"No, that's a no-go area for Zac, but Eric is not nearly as gentle as Marcus. Zac's head needs to be in the right place to deal with him."

Dale frowned. He didn't like the idea of any man playing with Zac let alone one who was known to be a committed sadist. "He's experiencing a lot of firsts. They should be with someone who understands him."

"Yes, they should." Luke's pale gaze drilled into Dale. He held his hands up.

"Whoa. You can't possibly be thinking it should be me. Zac is so far out of my league he might as well be on Mars."

"Why," Tor questioned, "because he's rich? Because his father is one of the most powerful businessmen in America? Or because you're afraid to get too close because you're in danger of falling for him?"

"I need another drink after all." Dale grabbed the wine bottle and filled his glass again. "I'm going to regret this, but I don't care." He took a deep swallow. "Those are all perfectly valid reasons for not encouraging him."

"From what I've seen," Luke said, "he doesn't need much encouragement where you're concerned."

"I can't believe the two of you are ganging up on me. I thought you'd be warning me off."

"We want what's best for Zac."

"I'm a lifestyle Dom," Dale said, "not someone who plays for fun every now and again. I can't turn it off and on again, something I'm certain you both understand."

Tor collected up the dishes. "I don't think Zac's submission is something that he saves up for evenings out, Dale. He may as well have 'sub' tattooed on his ass."

"You shouldn't be thinking about his backside," Dale growled.

"And there we go."

Dale scrubbed a hand through his close-cropped hair. "So what do you expect me to do about it?"

"Nothing yet," Luke said. "Let's see how it goes with Eric tomorrow. I have a feeling that Zac will be the one to make the next move."

Dale massaged his temples, the start of a headache showing its face. "After this conversation, there had better be some more really good puddings in my future."

Luke and Tor both laughed. "Okay, enough of the third degree. Let's have coffee and go talk about new acquisitions for the dungeon."

Dale heaved a sigh of relief. "That sounds like a much safer topic. Why can't being kinky be easy?"

"Mixing psychology, emotion, motivation and men... Never going to be an easy combination," Luke said.

"You're not kidding. I'll be much happier contributing to the debate on the relative merits of suede or leather on the top of a spanking bench," Dale said as he shoved his chair back. "Dungeon equipment has to be more straightforward."

"That sounds all kinds of wrong," Tor said, chuckling. "I'll go make coffee. You should break out the brandy, Luke, I think Dale might need it, hangover notwithstanding."

Chapter Fourteen

Zac gave the chains holding him in place an experimental tug. The cuffs around his wrists were snug but not cutting into his skin. He was as comfortable as he could be considering he was naked and chained to a dungeon wall. He watched, intrigued, as Eric tested the weight of a number of different whips and floggers. The slight furrow between his brows increased when he wasn't happy with the heft or the balance. Zac was more interested in how the strands would feel against his skin.

Eric Walcott couldn't be more different to Marcus. He'd arrived on a powerful motorbike, clad head to toe in black leather. When he'd taken off his helmet, a cascade of dreadlocks had tumbled around his shoulders. He'd taken one look at Zac, waiting nervously at the door, and drawn him into a rough hug.

"You'll more than do. I want you in the dungeon. Naked."

Zac had been so taken aback, he couldn't do anything but comply. He'd caught sight of Luke's knowing grin as he'd shown Eric the concealed doorway that led to the dungeon steps. He must have known that Eric wasn't backward about coming forward. It certainly hadn't taken him long to remove Zac's clothes.

"I'm going to warm your skin a little, get you relaxed and wanting," Eric said, running a finger down Zac's torso. "I'm not the kind of Dom who will talk your ear off. I prefer action. You know Luke's here to make sure I behave myself?" He had a sultry West Indian accent that was all sex.

"Yes, Sir." Zac didn't know where Luke was standing but he was glad he was around.

When Eric stripped off his jacket and T-shirt he revealed a set of abs that Zac could only dream of achieving. Realizing that his mouth was open, Zac clamped his lips together. *Holy shit, he's ripped.*

"Pretty." Eric pinched one of Zac's nipples. "Need to get some clamps on these."

"Oh God," Zac moaned. Eric was moving fast, and it was all a bit overwhelming.

"I'm not the religious type, but I'll have you worshipping my cock before the day is out. Gonna hurt you so good." Eric slapped the strands of the flogger against his leather-wrapped thigh. "This one will do." He whirled the strands in a figure-of-eight, cutting swathes through the air. Drifts of breeze caressed Zac's body and despite the cool temperature in the dungeon, he was sweating. His erection drooped. Eric cracked his knuckles and took up a stance side-on to Zac, doing a few more experimental sweeps of the flogger.

Zac couldn't grab hold of a single logical thought. Visions of Dale filled his head, and he knew at that moment that the only man he wanted to do this to him was outside, digging in the dirt.

"Red," he whispered, at once ashamed and relieved. "Red."

Eric had him unchained and wrapped in a blanket in under a minute. He carried him out of the small cell and into the main room of the dungeon where he settled onto a chair and pulled Zac onto his lap. For a while he held him close without saying anything. Tears trickled down Zac's cheeks.

"I'll leave you together," Luke murmured from somewhere close by.

"Good boy." Eric petted Zac's hair.

"I'm sorry," Zac snuffled against Eric's chest.

"What for? Frankly, I'm surprised it took you as long as it did."

"You thought I'd use my safe word? Why?"

"Because Luke told me you would."

"I don't understand."

"When I chained you to that wall, you were hard but you were a thousand miles away. Who were you thinking about?"

Zac didn't respond. He didn't want to admit what he guessed Eric already knew.

"The moment you focused on me, you went soft. You weren't into the situation anymore. It was a case of how long, not when. I would have stood there whirling that flogger around like an idiot until the end of the day without ever touching you if I had to."

Zac took a shuddering breath. "I'm sorry I wasted your time."

"You didn't. I had a great ride down here on the bike. I got to admire a beautiful young man wearing my chains. I fully intend to take advantage of Tor's cooking before I head back to London and if anything I've done has helped you get things straight in your head, I count that a success."

"I don't know what to say. Thank you, I guess."

"Why don't you get dressed then you and I will go pay Luke a visit and let him know that things need to change? We'll get some hot tea into you because you are probably a bit shocked."

"Do all you Brits think tea is the answer to everything?"

"Hey, I'm Jamaican but I've been here since I was five—long enough to catch the addiction. Never diss the benefits of tea within hearing of a Brit because they'll probably expel you from the country. That's my sage advice for the day." He helped Zac to his feet then left him alone to dress.

Zac gave himself a quick rub down with a towel before pulling on the clothes he had not long taken off. He massaged the back of his neck with one hand. "What a fucking mess."

"Are you ready?" Eric wandered over to him. "I was just taking a proper look around this space. Outside of The Underground, I think it's the best equipped dungeon I've ever seen. I'm definitely going to have to get myself back here for some fun times."

Zac couldn't help but smile at Eric's enthusiasm. "I really am sorry that it couldn't be with me."

"Not everyone could turn down all this hotness, you know." Eric swept a hand down his body, now covered by a clinging black T-shirt. He slapped his own abs. "You enjoyed the tough guy act, though, didn't you?"

"The bike, the leather..."

"Oh, that's genuine enough. But I'm also into amateur dramatics and knitting. Did you really think

The Retreat would give you to someone extreme after Marcus? Though he's far too much of a gentleman for my taste, compared to him I'm hard-core."

"I'm new to all this. I have no clue about anything. You were believable, that's for sure."

"I'll take that. Ready to go upstairs and face the music?"

Zac nodded. "I think so but I feel like an idiot."

"Safe words are there for a reason, Zac. You should never feel stupid for using yours. It's not something you did lightly. I could see the conflict in your eyes. For a while I thought you might actually let me flog you."

"Would you have, I mean if I hadn't said anything? Or if I'd begged you to?"

Eric shook his head. "I've been in the lifestyle a long time. I can recognize when someone's not into a scene. I'm glad you did say red, though—much better for you to make the decision and understand that you're in control and safe."

Eric led the way up the narrow stone steps and through the concealed door into the corridor. They walked through to the banqueting hall and found Luke already seated at the table, a pot of tea and three mugs laid out next to a plate of biscuits. Eric gave Zac a little nudge to get him moving.

"Don't look so worried, Zac. You haven't done anything wrong." Luke gave him a welcoming smile. "Take a seat."

Eric pulled a chair out for him, and Zac slumped into it. "I've already tried to tell him that he's not at fault," Eric said. "Excellent, Bourbons. Love 'em."

Luke poured tea, added milk then pushed the mug toward Zac. "A hot drink will make you feel better."

"I'm sorry to be such a flake. I know a lot of work has gone into planning my stay."

"Plans are made to be changed," Luke said. Zac avoided his gaze, Luke's shrewd scrutiny made him want to squirm. "Look at me, Zac. You have nothing to be ashamed of. You're not putting anyone out and nobody is upset with you. I asked Eric to put on the big bad Dom act this morning deliberately to make you think hard about what you really wanted."

"And it worked," Zac said. He followed Eric's example and dunked a biscuit in his tea. "Not that I didn't appreciate Eric in all that leather, because yum." Eric grinned. "But it wasn't Eric's face I was seeing down there."

"It was Dale, wasn't it?" Luke suggested.

Zac didn't need to verbalize an answer, it was clear Luke, Eric and probably everyone else at The Retreat knew what was in his head better than he did. The tea warmed him and gradually some of the tension eased from his shoulders. "So what happens now?"

"You and I have a detailed conversation about you stripping off for other men."

Zac whipped his head around as Dale stalked toward him. "We do?"

"Yes, we do."

A tiny flame of hope lit in Zac's heart.

"You're in trouble now, boy," Eric said, laughing. "Morning, Dale."

Dale rolled his eyes. "Not helping, Eric. Let's take a walk, Zac."

Zac got to his feet consumed by anxiety and hope. It was clear that Dale had come in from the garden as he was dressed in his work clothes. He must have moved fast because he still had his boots on. There was a smear of mud across one cheek, and his hands were ingrained with dirt. To Zac he looked perfect.

Dale led the way outside, and Zac followed, feet dragging a little. In the courtyard, he took a deep breath of fresh air, filling his lungs. His skin felt too tight.

"Don't be angry with me."

"Why on earth would I be angry?" Dale sounded surprised.

"I tried really hard not to think about you, but it was no good. It was Eric down there in the dungeon with me, but I could only see your face. I couldn't carry on. It wasn't fair to Eric. It would have been dishonest, and I didn't want him to touch me. I wanted it to be you."

"I'm glad." They strolled across the lawn toward the trees.

"You are?"

"You have no idea how hard it's been for me to keep my hands off you. I hated watching you with Marcus, and when Eric arrived... I'd have quite happily punched him in the face and dragged you away but it wasn't my place to do that. This wasn't supposed to happen, Zac. The Doms visiting have been especially selected to give you the best possible introduction to the lifestyle in a safe environment. They're good men. I know Eric from The Underground and he's a highly respected Dom and a good man."

"He's gorgeous." Zac held up his hands as he caught Dale's side eye. "Hey, I can appreciate a good-looking man. But he's not you."

"We've only known each other a few days."

"I know, and that's why I'm so sure. I've never come across anyone who's affected me so quickly, not in the way you have."

Dale grunted. "Same."

"So, when you were ordering me around in the garden…"

"It was the closest I could get to being your Dom. I wanted to test how you responded, and I wasn't disappointed, but it made things worse, not better. Then yesterday at the apartment, Christ, you're a test of a man's willpower."

"I wanted to suck you so bad. Having you lying there on the bed, skin all shiny, those incredible tattoos… I swear my balls were on fire. I wanted nothing more than for you to throw me down and fuck me for being impertinent."

"I wanted to spank you first." Dale held out his hand, and Zac took it like a lifeline. Dale's rough, work-hardened skin against his own softer fingers felt exactly right. "What a pair we are, neither of us have communication skills worth a damn."

"So what happens now?" Zac asked.

"I guess that's up to you. I'll support you, whatever you decide but I think you need to talk to Luke. If you want me to be there with you, then I will."

"I want to cancel the rest of the visiting Doms. I want to ask Luke if you can take their place for the rest of my stay. I want you to teach me, to show me…everything."

"Tor might have something to say about the unfinished extension to the kitchen garden."

"I don't think he'll mind. Do you?"

"No, in fact in the interests of full disclosure both Luke and Tor had noticed that there might be something growing between us."

"I talked to Skye and Rayne about it too. We were going to come up with a plan that would bring the two of us together, but I don't think that's needed now."

"That's a relief. I can only imagine the kind of mischief the three of you would have gotten up to. Rayne will definitely be disappointed."

Zac chuckled. "He told me his middle name was 'mayhem'."

"Sounds about right. But you'd have gone along with whatever he cooked up?"

"I'm not going to incriminate myself by admitting that." The grass was wet, and Zac's shoes and the bottoms of his trousers were getting damp. The breeze was chillier than it had been the last few days, and he shivered. Dale stripped off his sweatshirt and wrangled Zac into it. It smelt of earth and leaves and Dale.

"Thank you." They'd reached the boundary wall, and Zac turned back to look at the house. A light mist had formed blurring the edges of the building. "Do you think it's haunted? All those Gothic turrets and crenulations... If there's any justice, it should have a ghost or two at least."

"Not that I've heard, but I bet if you listen closely you can hear the echo of distant screaming in the dungeon." Dale grinned.

"You're laughing at me."

"Maybe a bit. You don't watch those awful sham ghost hunting programs do you?"

"Does *Ghostbusters* count?"

"I'll give you that one. We should go back, talk to Luke. You're cold, and I guess you haven't eaten much today either."

"I wasn't hungry this morning. I was too nervous waiting for Eric to arrive."

"I get growly when I think about you and him together in the dungeon."

Zac looped his arm through Dale's. "I love that you do. How about I promise not to get naked for anyone but you from now on?"

"If you're with me, that's not up for debate. No one but me gets to touch you."

Zac gave a short laugh. "So possessive. Did you know that Luke had warned Eric I might not be up for playing with him? Honestly, he spent so long whirling that flogger without touching me, his arm must ache. I made him wait far too long for my safe word."

"The rest of your firsts should be with me. First flogging, first spanking."

"First fucking… Please?"

Dale gave Zac's ass a soft smack. "Try stopping me."

"I don't want to. Just the thought of having you inside me gets me hard and aching."

Dale stuck a hand down the front of his trousers and adjusted himself. "You should stop talking now."

"Or what?"

"Or I find a nice big ball gag and shut you up. It would have been preferable not to have to stand in front of Luke with a hard-on."

"Sorry."

"You're not sorry at all and for that you'll have to be punished."

Zac gulped. He got the feeling that Dale wasn't kidding, and his head filled with all kinds of potential scenarios, none of which included him getting off. "I can add stuff to my red list, can't I? Dale?" The gleam in Dale's eyes was feral. All of a sudden, Eric and his flogger didn't seem like such a bad option.

Chapter Fifteen

As much as Dale would have liked to take Zac straight to one of The Retreat's well-appointed bedrooms, he resisted. Though he was convinced that Zac had worked out what he needed, Dale wanted to give him time to get things settled in his head. Zac had gone from facing down Eric, and his flogger, in the dungeon to admitting his feelings in the space of a morning. Things were moving at light speed, and for his own sanity, Dale need to slow them down. Not for himself because he'd never been more sure of anything in his life, but Zac was bright and shiny new to the lifestyle and shouldn't be rushed.

"It's only polite that we have lunch with Eric considering he came all this way." Dale led Zac through the banqueting hall to the staff dining room. He didn't take back his sweatshirt because Zac was adorable, swamped in its folds, fingertips barely peeking from the ends of the sleeves. Not that Zac seemed inclined to relinquish it anyway. When they walked into the room, the chatter subsided into silence. Skye, who was sitting in Luke's lap, arms looped around Luke's neck, stared at them, eyes wide. Tor smirked, then gave Rayne a quick clip round the ear, apparently to stop him gaping. Eric smiled, a picture of serenity as he sipped from a glass of juice.

"Well, this isn't awkward much," Dale said, tucking Zac against his side.

"You're very welcome to join us for lunch." It was Luke who broke the silence.

"We thought you'd have Zac bent over the nearest flat surface by now," Rayne blurted out.

Zac's face went scarlet, and Dale would lay odds that the rest of his body was just as pink

"You are in so much trouble, young man," Tor growled. "You, me, dungeon, now."

"But… What about lunch?"

"Food should be the last thing on your mind, you little brat. I'm sure Skye can serve without your help." Tor got to his feet, grabbed a handful of Rayne's copper hair and yanked him to the door. Skye's face betrayed his concern, but he clearly caught Rayne's grin at the same time as Dale and shrugged. He slithered from Luke's lap. "I'll go fetch the food then since the kitchen staff have better things to do." He beamed.

Once Tor and a mildly protesting Rayne had left the room, Dale pulled out a chair for Zac before sitting next to him. Zac wasn't looking at anyone, just staring at the table. Dale cupped the nape of Zac's neck. "There's no need to be embarrassed. I *was* pretty much contemplating what Rayne described but I have a better brain to mouth filter than he does. In fact, his is nonexistent."

"Really? You were thinking about… Oh God, me too!" Zac wiggled on his seat while Eric snorted his amusement and Luke ran his fingers through his hair and tried not to smile. After that, the mood became more relaxed, and they chatted over a delicious lunch of soup and sandwiches.

"Which room are you going to use?" Skye asked. "They're all prepared, so you can choose."

"The garage apartment, I assumed," Dale said.

"Oh no! You have to try out one of the bedrooms," Skye exclaimed. "Tell him, Sir!"

"As Skye has made sure they're all ready for you, Dale, then you should take advantage."

"Then I think I'll leave the choice up to Zac as I haven't had the tour," Dale said. "I'm sure they're all amazing."

"I'm not sure I can remember them very well," Zac said. "I saw so much on my first day it was hard to take it all in. I recall bits and pieces but I'd probably get them all mixed up."

"I can help," Skye said, giving Luke an appealing glance.

"Go ahead, sweetheart. You know the rooms better than all of us." Luke's pride was evident.

Skye sat up straighter. "Okay, so if you stand on the main staircase and look up at the gallery, there are five bedrooms, all color-themed. From left to right they are blue, red, gold, gray and green. Zac has been staying in the green room."

"I think we can rule that one out," Dale said, not wanting to think about Marcus and Zac sharing a bed, even if they had only slept in it.

"Each of the rooms has the most wonderful kinky secrets," Skye continued, "and they're fun to discover but to give you a few ideas, the blue room has a sling in the canopy of the four poster, there's an amazing black-tiled bathroom in the red room and a cage under the bed, the gold room has a genuine priests' hole and there's an amazing bungee wall in there."

Next to Dale, Zac was bouncing his leg until Dale rested a hand on his thigh and gave him a reassuring grin. "Sounds exciting, doesn't it?"

"Uh huh."

"Use your words, Zac."

"A bit too exciting, Sir."

"Ah. Do carry on, Skye."

Skye gave a soft giggle. "The footboard of the bed in the gray room converts to a set of stocks and in the green room there's a chair…" He blushed. "The seat flips over and there's a fixed dildo…to sit on."

Zac's gulp was audible. *Pretty sure I could get that chair moved.* Dale had no problem imagining Zac tied to the chair, tormented and unable to move. "That has potential," he murmured. Zac gave a strangled moan. "Like that idea, don't you, boy?" Zac shook his head a bit harder than necessary. "Lying to your Dom isn't a good idea, Zac. Thanks, Skye, that was enlightening. I think Zac and I should go take advantage of the facilities now."

"If you want to use the dungeon later," Luke said, "I'll make sure it's ready for you. I can't imagine Tor will need it for too long."

"Oh, I don't know," Dale mused, "seems like Rayne could take quite a while to deal with. We won't be using the dungeon today so no need to evict them." Luke nodded and seemed happy with that decision. Dale turned to Zac. "Are you ready?"

"I am." Zac reached for Dale's hand, though there was no uncertainty in his voice.

Dale tried to recall Skye's words as he led Zac up the main staircase. "The gold room is the one in the middle, isn't it?"

"That's right. You're not going to put me in the priest's hole, are you?"

"If I do, it'll be because that's what will give me pleasure." Dale opened the door, finding the key on the inside. He gave Zac a little tug to bring him inside then closed the door. He took in his surroundings, wondering at the level of luxury. There was an ornate Turkish rug on the floor and a room-height mirror set on one wall. Curious, Dale walked over to it and soon found the button that activated a mechanism, which swiveled the mirror through one hundred and eighty degrees to reveal a padded surface crisscrossed by a lattice of bungee cords attached to hooks at the sides. "Nice," he murmured. "Carey spared no expense with this place." The bed was huge, with a scrollwork cast-iron headboard and metal posts at the bottom corners. Piles of colorful pillows were mounded at one end, and the cover was a beautiful shade of antique gold. On further exploration, Dale discovered that the bed was made up with sheets and blankets rather than a duvet.

"It's beautiful, isn't it, Sir?" Zac was still standing just inside the door.

"It is, and so are you." Zac blushed easily, delicate pink shading his sharp cheekbones. He cast his eyes down, displaying his thick dark lashes to their full effect. Looking at him was enough to make Dale hard. "Take your clothes off, Zac. Fold them and put them on the chair in the corner then present yourself."

Dale had taken his boots off when he'd returned to the house after walking outside with Zac, and he'd given Zac his fleece so he was left wearing his work trousers and T-shirt. He stripped off his socks then checked the back of his trousers to make sure they weren't dirty. He didn't want to sit on the bed covers and leave mud and grass all over the place. He put the level of luxury out of his head, nudging aside the feeling that he shouldn't be there. It was furniture — everyone used it. He climbed onto the bed then arranged the pillows in a way to suit him. Once he was satisfied, he leaned back to watch Zac undress. It was a show men would pay to view. Even though Dale had seen Zac naked before, it hadn't been under such deliberate circumstances not with the promise of even better things to come.

Zac got down to his underwear before he met Dale's gaze. His shorts were tented and after he'd removed them, he tried to cover himself with his hands.

"When I say present yourself, Zac, I want you to stand feet apart with your hands behind your head. I'll give you a pass this time because my instructions may not have been clear enough." Dale licked his lips as he admired Zac's lean body and rigid erection. It was hard to believe that Zac was willing to give himself over to Dale's control. *I think I'm dreaming and I don't want to wake up.* "Good. Now come sit here with me." He patted the spot between his legs.

Zac scrambled into place, leaning back against Dale's chest. Dale felt the heat from his skin through the thin fabric of his T-shirt. He wrapped his arms around Zac's body, holding him tight. Zac let his head rest on Dale's shoulder. "I guess you're used to surroundings like these?" Dale asked.

"Sure, but those places belong to my dad's friends. They aren't me and they aren't where I want to be."

"Where *do* you want to be?"

"With you. Wherever that might be. That's okay, isn't it?"

"More than. Later I'm going to take you back to the apartment over the garages. This room has given me some great ideas, but domination isn't about all this stuff. It's a state of mind."

"The state of mind I'm in when I'm naked and you're not?"

Dale brushed his hand across one of Zac's nipples. "It's a demonstration. When you give control to me, your body becomes mine to do with as I please. Pain or pleasure — both are in my gift." Zac shivered but his erection didn't waver. "I want to put that eager cock of yours in a cage, put my cuffs around your wrists and ankles and a collar around your neck. I want to play with you until you're incoherent with need, begging for release, then torment you some more." He paused. "Just thinking about all the things I want to do to you keeps me as hard as iron."

"Will you let me do something about that this time?" Zak twisted in Dale's hold until he had turned around and was straddling Dale's thighs. He rested one hand on Dale's crotch. "Please, Sir?" He didn't wait for a response but deftly tackled the button on Dale's waistband until Dale grasped his wrists.

"You don't have to do this, Zac."

"Try and stop me...unless you want to use *your* safe word, that is?" He shook his hands free and continued where he left off until he gained access to Dale's cock.

"Brat." Dale's cock was thick and heavy. "You've been spending too much time around Rayne. You're walking a very fine line." *I should stop him but I don't think I can.*

"You can spank me later." Zac reached out a tentative hand to stroke Dale's shaft. "How can something so hard be so soft? It's like the skin of a ripe peach." Fluid oozed from the tip. Zac flicked his tongue out for a taste then licked his lips. "Mmm, salty." He took the first inch into his mouth and lapped with his tongue. He pressed lightly down with his teeth, peeking at Dale from beneath his lashes.

Dale moaned and clenched his buttocks. "You've been practicing."

Zac pulled off with a slurp. "Should have found a bigger zucchini." He grinned.

"Oh, you just guaranteed that spanking."

Zac took him a little deeper, tickling his balls a little at the same time, and Dale swore creatively. The heat of Zac's mouth surrounded him, and every tiny contact of his tongue was sending thrills down Dale's spine in uncontrollable waves. Zac grasped Dale's thighs to get better purchase and ducked his head. Gradually he picked up his pace, manipulating the velvety sheath by clamping his lips down.

Dale was barely coherent but managed to indicate his imminent release.

"Coming. Now! Let. Go."

Zac shook his head, and the additional movement took Dale over the edge. His back arched like a bow as he pulsed deep into Zac's throat, shuddering from head to toe. When the spasms stopped, Zac slid away from him with a shy smile. He remained on his knees, and Dale fixed hungry eyes on his body. He reached out and tangled his fingers into glossy waves, pulling Zac's head down so that he could reach to claim his mouth. Zac's lips were soft and warm, ripe for bruising. He tasted sweet. Addictive. His low whimpers were distracting in the best way.

After giving Zac a suitably thorough kissing, Dale zipped up then replumped the pillows. Zac remained sprawled across his lap, facing him.

"We need to discuss your contract."

"Or we could kiss some more."

"Contract first."

"I'd rather discuss my need to come" Zac batted his eyelashes and gave his erection a pointed stare, making Dale laugh.

"I'm sure you would, but I don't think that's going to happen any time soon."

"I already signed a contract with The Retreat. Is that not enough?"

"The situation has changed somewhat. I haven't seen your list of limits yet, and you'll be spending more time with me than you would have been with any of the visiting Doms so we need to talk about it before we go any further."

"I want to make it absolutely clear that orgasms were not included in my hard or medium or soft or any kind of limits, Sir." Zac's hand strayed toward his cock.

"Noted. Do you want me to tie your hands behind your back while we talk?"

Zac moved his hand away. "No thank you, Sir."

"So what were your hard limits?"

"I kind of left most things open because I have so little experience. I don't know what I do or don't like yet, but there are a few things that in my head are a bit icky, so I guess those are as close as I get to hard limits. I don't want you peeing on me, Sir."

"I generally prefer to use the bathroom myself," Dale said. "That can't be everything."

"No permanent body modification, tattoos or piercings. It's not that I'm against them, in fact I think tattoos are as hot as hell." Zac traced one of the dark lines running around Dale's bicep. "But if that's going to happen, I want it to be with my forever Dom."

"Fair enough." Dale could imagine the rush of having his designs etched on Zac's pristine skin. "Anything else?" Zac didn't reply. "Zac?"

"Oh, sorry. Got a bit distracted thinking about you watching while some guy tattooed my butt with 'Property of Dale'."

"Jesus." Dale dug his fingernails into his palm to stop himself throwing Zac onto his back for a rough fucking.

"Oh, I don't think I'll be into heavy pain. I don't want to be so incapacitated after a scene that I can't enjoy myself."

"From what you're saying, I think we'll be a good fit. I'm a sadist, but more interested in denial than inflicting pain."

"But there's a difference between erotic pain and punishment, right?"

"Oh yes, punishment isn't meant to be fun. A spanking can be intensely erotic, though, and that is something I enjoy. A lot."

Zac squirmed. "Are you sure you wouldn't like to reconsider letting me come, Sir?"

"Sadist, remember?"

Dale was about to turn Zac over his lap when the room phone rang. "This had better be impending Armageddon-level important," he muttered as he picked up the receiver. "This is Dale."

"I'm sorry to disturb you, Dale. I can't tell you how much." It was Luke. "But you need to come downstairs to the staff dining room. Eric caught our drone pilot."

"Well, fuck." Dale stared heavenward. "Someone up there hates me. I'm on my way, Luke. Give me a few minutes."

"Don't tell me you have to go," Zac pleaded.

"Luke needs me for something, but I'll be as quick as I can and when I get back, I'll tell you all about it. There shouldn't be any secrets between us and there are a few things I need to tell you before we get to know each other better. Or rather, my hand gets acquainted with your backside. Get under the covers so you don't get cold."

"Should I come with you?"

"No need. I won't be long. You stay cuddled in there—good motivation for me to be quick. No touching your dick."

"So not fair."

As he left the room, Dale didn't dare look back. His willpower wasn't nearly strong enough to resist Zac, burrowing under the covers, tousled and needy.

Chapter Sixteen

Dale jogged all the way to the staff dining room with no idea what to expect when he got there. He realized halfway down the stairs that his feet were still bare, but there was little point in turning around. When he went into the room, everyone currently residing at The Retreat apart from Zac was seated around the table. This included Eric, attired in full biker leathers, and a stranger, who Dale assumed was the drone pilot.

"He's just a kid!" Dale blurted out. He wasn't sure what he'd been expecting, but it wasn't the waiflike, blue-eyed blond hunched in the seat next to Eric.

"I'm twenty-one," the blond muttered without looking up.

"You, keep quiet. You're in enough trouble as it is," Eric said.

"I said I was sorry."

"One more word and I'll gag you."

"You wouldn't."

"Would."

Luke gave an exasperated sigh. "You two are giving me a headache. Dale, I'd like you to meet Aaron Scott, our mystery drone pilot, and I'd love your opinion on what we should do with him. Aaron, why don't you tell Dale what you've been up to?"

"Who's he?"

"Never you mind."

"I already..." Aaron clearly caught Luke's gimlet stare and absorbed the inherent threat. "Fine. I just want my drone back. Well, it's not mine, it's my older brother's, and he's going to do serious physical damage to my person if I don't return it."

"How about you start from the beginning," Dale said, "because you've pulled me away from a place where my mind was engaged in far more pleasant things, and I need you to give me the idiot's guide because my brain is scrambled."

At Tor's side, Rayne sniggered and received a clip around the ear for his trouble. He gave Tor a baleful glare.

"I only wanted to see what was going on in here," Aaron began to explain. "I hacked the website, for this place that is... It's a bit of an urban myth in what passes for the kink scene around here, and I was curious. You've no idea what it's like, buried down here in the countryside where New Forest ponies outnumber gay Dominants by about a thousand to one. Honestly, in this day and age, you'd think there'd be more out and proud Dommy types wandering around, but no. I have bigger dry spells than California."

"Could you stick to the point...? Please." Dale wasn't averse to begging if it got Aaron back on track.

"I hacked the website, like I said, and it was enticing so I wanted to take a look at The Retreat. Not my fault

I was tempted. It sounds amazing but there was no way I was ever going to get inside, the security here is like Alcatraz. Of course I realize that Alcatraz isn't a prison anymore, it's a tourist attraction, but I've seen the film, the one with Charlie Hunnam, not the earlier one, and he's very hot by the way."

Dale caught himself growling under his breath. Tor looked like he wanted to throttle someone and wasn't particular about who it might be. Rayne was grinning, and Skye was eyeing Luke with some trepidation.

"Get. On. With. It." Dale was in Tor's camp.

"Sorry, so I decided to borrow Henry, that's my brother's drone that he got for his birthday. It was really expensive, and the whole family clubbed together to get it for him cos he's into photography and isn't much good at anything else. I managed to fly it over the wall and get it back okay the first time, but then the second time it crashed into something, and I couldn't get it back. Bummer."

"It crashed into me, you idiot," Dale said.

"Sorry, yeah, really sorry. Don't hit me, okay?"

"I'm not going to hit you, though the idea has merit."

"That's good because I think my brother will. I need the drone back so I can get it fixed. He's gonna pound me anyway." Aaron sounded mournful but not very remorseful.

Dale didn't know whether to laugh or take a paddle to Aaron's backside. He guessed he might have to hand over the latter duty. "So you weren't looking for someone in particular?"

"Of course not, that would be invasion of privacy," Aaron said.

"Lord save me." Dale looked around the room to see if there was any alcohol to hand because he suddenly felt the need for a stiff drink.

"I thought I could sneak inside when the gates opened for his motorbike — cool model by the way — and look for my drone." He flapped a hand at Eric.

"And how did you think you'd get out again?" Eric asked.

Aaron shrugged. "I didn't think that far ahead. Hey, now that I'm here, do you have any jobs going?"

"Unbelievable," Dale said, knowing that he sounded like a grumpy old man. "I suggest you let Eric deal with him, Luke. Give him the drone back, after wiping the memory card, and get him to report back here for a suitable punishment."

"That sounds like the perfect solution," Tor said. "Punishment definitely needs to be part of the solution. You also need to write down exactly how you hacked the website, so that we can make sure it never happens again."

"I'd be more than happy to come back here and assist as needed," Eric said, smirking. Aaron gazed up at him with adoring eyes.

"Do you always wear leather?"

"More often than you might think," Eric said.

"Wow. Yum."

"A little more remorse on your part wouldn't go amiss, Aaron," Luke said. "I get the feeling that you've achieved exactly what you set out to. You need to be aware that you could have killed someone flying that drone. I can think of several laws you've broken and we'd be well within our rights to take you to the nearest police station and leave you to the tender mercies of the law."

"Please don't do that," Aaron said. "I honestly didn't mean any harm. I'm really sorry that someone got hurt. I'll come back and wash dishes or scrub floors, whatever you want."

Skye grabbed Aaron's hand and gave it a squeeze. "Don't get upset. No one's going to hand you over to the police, I promise. You shouldn't be mean, Sir."

Aaron's eyes widened. "Why are you calling him Sir?"

"If you hacked the website, Aaron, that's a stupid question," Rayne said. "You know this is a BDSM retreat and it sounds like you know something about the lifestyle too."

"You mean the myths are true?" Aaron gaped.

"Close your mouth, boy, or I'll shove a ball gag in it," Eric said, pushing his chair back. "I've got a spare helmet. I'll take you and the drone home."

Dale was finding it increasingly difficult to focus on the conversation. It was clear that Eric found Aaron appealing, and Dale was more than happy to leave arrangements for Aaron's punishment, whatever that might be, to Eric and Luke. "If nobody objects, I'm going back upstairs. I have unfinished business of my own to deal with."

Rayne snorted with laughter.

"One trip to the dungeon today wasn't enough for you, brat?" Tor snapped.

Rayne smirked, Aaron went scarlet and Dale took it as his cue to leave.

"Thanks, Dale, we'll catch up in the morning," Luke said. "If nothing else, the mystery is solved, and I don't think we have to worry about any kidnap plots for the time being."

"Kidnap plots?" Skye turned to Luke, and Dale took the path of least resistance and left as quickly as possible. There was no way he wanted to get between Skye and Luke if they were about to discuss Luke hiding things from his adoring sub. He trudged back up the stairs, pausing at the door to the gold room to compose himself. The conversation he was about to have was likely to be just as tough.

Zac nestled beneath the bed covers, wishing Dale would return. He'd started missing him as soon as he'd gone out of the door and craved his strong, certain presence. He was self-aware enough to recognize how scattered he was after the events of the day and didn't want to be alone. Things with Dale weren't progressing nearly as fast as he would have liked, but Zac appreciated Dale's patience and care. Sucking Dale's cock had been a sublime experience and something that he couldn't wait to repeat. Everything about it had been perfect, and now he had the slight ache in his jaw to remind him of the stretch from Dale's girth. The taste of him lingered on Zac's tongue, his scent still invaded his nostrils. He breathed deeply, wanting as much of Dale inside him as possible.

He was curious about what Luke could want that was so important but more out of concern that it might take Dale away from him than anything. He couldn't think of anything involving the garden that was urgent, but maybe he wasn't seeing the whole picture. *Dale wouldn't have gone if he didn't think he needed to.*

The moment the door opened, Zac sat bolt upright, the covers pooling around his hips. "Is everything all right? What's going on?"

Dale strolled across the room. He sat next to Zac on the bed, staying on top of the covers. "I don't trust myself to get in there with you until I've told you everything. A D/s relationship is about trust, and we shouldn't continue while there are things you don't know about me."

"You're scaring me."

"I'd appreciate you letting me speak until I've finished, then I'll answer any questions you have, but I need to get this out in one go, okay?"

Zac wanted nothing more than to scramble into Dale's lap and give him a hug, but he nodded, not trusting himself to speak. Dale sounded so serious.

"First of all, I need you to know that I am genuinely a landscape gardener, but extending Tor's kitchen garden is not the real reason for me being here."

"It's not? Sorry—keeping quiet now."

"Your father, Carey Hoffman and Luke were all concerned for your safety while you're here what with the ongoing kidnap threat. You don't need to know exactly what I did in the army but let's just say that I'm well trained at blending into the background. I was asked to keep an eye on things, look out for anything suspicious and head off any possible threat. I've been working in the garden in the morning, sleeping in the late afternoon then patrolling at night."

"The ninja outfit! I should have known."

Dale shook his head. "I look nothing like a ninja. Lord help me, I'm never going to get this out. In the grounds the other day, I spotted a drone. The first time was when you and Marcus were walking together, when he was using the lead. It came back again when you were working with me, in fact it flew right into me.

You were in the shed at the time. It crashed and you didn't see it."

"Your shoulder...that was how you got that bruising."

Dale nodded. "I'm sorry I lied about how that happened. I was lucky that thing didn't take my head off. Needless to say, we all thought that the drone might be part of a plot to get to you." Dale ran his hand over his stubbly head. "It proved not to be the case. The reason I was called downstairs is that Eric found a boy outside the gates. He wanted his drone back."

Zac sniggered. He couldn't help himself. He pressed his lips together, trying not to laugh but caught the amused gleam in Dale's eyes. "Oh my God, I'm sorry. I know you're trying to have a serious talk with me, but that's too funny."

Dale shook his head. "Turns out this kid, well, young man, hacked The Retreat's website and let his curiosity get the better of him. According to him, Aaron, the kink scene down here in the forest is somewhat lacking."

Zac burst into laughter. "I can imagine. The area doesn't strike me as overly endowed with dungeons. So no one is trying to kidnap me?"

"Apparently not," Dale said. "Not the drone pilot at any rate. He's just in need of having his ass warmed."

"The Doms' answer to everything. So, from now on you won't need to go skulking around the grounds in the middle of the night?"

"Skulking? Makes *me* sound like a criminal."

"No more surveillance then, is that better?"

"Uh, no and yes."

"Then everything's good, isn't it?"

"You're not upset about not being in on this?"

"No, why should I be? I'm not in any way surprised that my dad put plans in place without telling me. He has a habit of doing that and there was no way that either you or I could possibly know that we'd end up together. That was fate at work."

"So, are we okay?"

"More than. Of course, things could be better…"

"How so?"

"You could be in here with me, naked."

"I think we have some unfinished business before that happens, young man."

Zac's cock, which had drooped a little, got back with the program. "I don't know what you mean." He hoped that acting innocent might encourage Dale to go easy on him.

"I want you across my lap."

"I…"

"The only appropriate response at this time, Zac, is 'yes, Sir'."

Zac shivered as he crawled out from beneath the covers and positioned himself across Dale's thighs. "A little further. I won't let you fall." When Zac was situated in the way Dale wanted, his head was over the side of the bed, and he could grip the bottom edge of the mattress. His cock poked between Dale's thighs, and his legs rested on the part of the bed he'd just vacated. It wasn't comfortable but Dale's hand on the small of his back let him know that he was in no danger of slipping off. When Dale touched his ass, Zac jerked then gave a nervous giggle. Dale stroked him, the touches gentle and soothing. He tapped Zac's inner thigh until he parted his legs wider.

"That's good. I'm going to spank you six times and when I'm done, you're going to thank me."

"Yes, Sir."

The first blow sent heat blooming across Zac's backside, his dick twitched, and he wanted more. Dale gave it to him, the blows getting progressively harder until the final one made Zac yelp.

"Thank you, Sir," he whispered. "More would be good, though."

"Maybe you should keep your thoughts to yourself, Zac," Dale said. "They could get you into trouble." He gave Zac two more hard smacks.

"Ow! I was thinking aloud, Sir. I really need to come."

"Did you mean to say that, because now I'm not sure?" Dale pushed his finger between Zac's ass cheeks to pat his hole.

"Yes!" Zac's voice came out at least an octave higher than usual. "I've never been more sure of anything in my life. Ever."

"And who gets to decide if and when you are allowed to come?"

"Sadly, you do, Sir." Zac suspected Dale was not yet in a giving mood.

"That's right." Dale helped Zac off his lap and back under the covers. "And that's not so sad for me. I'm rather enjoying myself."

"The sheets are rubbing my butt," Zac complained. The light ache and soreness were exciting.

"Then it's a good thing the thread count is so high. I could definitely be tempted to liberate some of this bed linen." Much to Zac's delight, Dale climbed off the bed then undressed as far as a pair of very snug black boxer briefs. "Are you licking your lips?" Dale slipped beneath the covers next to him.

"Maybe?" Zac moved as close as he could, drawn to Dale's side like a bee to pollen, the attraction primal and irresistible. "I'll get to come sometime, won't I?"

"Probably. You've had a big day—I wouldn't want to overwhelm you."

Zac gave Dale a hard stare. "You have a strange sense of humor, you know that?"

"Dom humor. The best kind."

"You know, there's nowhere in the world I'd rather be right now. Even if you are determined to keep me frustrated."

"Good to know because I've no intention of letting you be anywhere else." Dale pulled him even closer. "I'm going to play with your body until you scream." The words were a whispered promise, and Zac couldn't wait to find out exactly what they meant. For a while he was happy to doze, warm and contented.

Dale could come up with a thousand reasons why he shouldn't take things further with Zac but having warmed Zac's ass and felt the heat of his mouth around his cock, Dale was no longer in the mood for ethical debate. The future was uncertain. It was entirely possible that he and Zac might only have a short time together. They'd met through a peculiar set of circumstances, but the attraction was there, deep and burning hot. Dale wanted Zac badly, and Luke's earlier words about grasping the moment resonated. He wrapped his arms around a napping Zac and pressed against him, nuzzling and kissing his slender neck. Zac responded instantly, moaning his pleasure. Skin against skin was how things were meant to be. Dale wanted Zac naked, defenseless and needing as his permanent state. "I want you."

"I want you to have me," Zac murmured as he slung a leg across Dale's thighs. "I'll get on my knees and beg if you want me to."

"The visual is appealing, but not yet." Dale reveled in the thrill of possession as he touched and tormented. He learned Zac's body with his fingertips and palms, with gentle strokes and wicked pinches. Zac writhed and squirmed, moaning and whimpering at every contact, demanding more of everything.

Dale threw back the covers — Zac's skin was as hot as his own — gaining better access. He gave Zac's rigid dick a squeeze then palmed his balls, enjoying their weight. He sought Zac's hole with eager fingers, testing his resistance, dipping inside him the slightest bit.

"More, please!" Zac pleaded, bucking his hips.

"Not without lube," Dale growled. He pushed Zac down, then grabbed a couple of pillows to position beneath his lower back so that his hips were raised. "Open your legs," he ordered sharply before sliding out of bed to fetch some lube. He took a few seconds to pause and admire the view. Zac's breathing was fast and erratic. He reached for his cock, and Dale slapped his hand away.

"Again? Don't you dare touch what's mine without permission." He went to the bathroom for lube and when he returned Zac was fisting his cock.

"You seem to have a problem following instructions," Dale said.

"Sorry! Sorry...I couldn't help myself."

Those puppy eyes are going to cause me no end of trouble. Dale was grateful for the ready supply of restraints. He found leather cuffs looped through the headboard, pulled Zac's arms over his head then tied him in place. "That's a punishment you've earned."

Maintaining eye contact Dale stripped off his underwear and stood looking down on his prize. He savored the moment, teasing his cock with gentle strokes. Zac swallowed, his Adam's apple giving him away.

"Do you know how much I love that you're powerless? Lying there, desperate for my touch but forced to wait."

"I'd guess a whole lot."

"And you'd be right."

Zac's eyes widened as Dale climbed on to the bed and knelt between his thighs. He grasped Zac's waist then pulled him down the bed a few inches, the pillows lifted his ass further and his arms were stretched to their limit.

"I'm healthy, but until you see my test results with your own eyes, we use protection," Dale said as he peeled a condom from its shiny packet. He rolled it slowly down his length. "If you weren't tied down, I'd get you to do that with your mouth." A thick smear of lubrication added a wet shine that glinted in the dim light. "Another time I'll get you to prep yourself while I watch or better still keep you plugged so that you're ready for me." He lifted Zac's legs so that his calves rested on Dale's shoulders. Zac whimpered. Pink stained his cheekbones, and his eye glittered. Dale longed to take him hard and fast but there was no way he was going to hurt Zac. *Getting rough can wait for another time.* He spent a long time stretching and teasing him until Zac was reduced to incoherent begging, though his pleading had little effect on Dale.

"One last chance to use your safe word." Dale pressed the tip of his sheathed cock against Zac's entrance. The resistance was a personal challenge.

Zac tugged hard on his bonds. "Do it!"

Dale didn't hesitate. With a single slow but persistent thrust, he buried himself to the hilt. Zac's internal muscles spasmed at the unaccustomed invasion and gripped him tightly. Dale stilled, resisting the desperate urge to pound Zac's ass but he'd already been sadistic enough. He could have been gentler. Zac's neck was corded in a silent scream, his bounds hands fisted, but slowly he relaxed. Tears rolled down his cheeks, and he smiled.

"God, so full!"

"One word from you, and I stop. Is it too much?" Dale thumbed away a tear.

"Burns…but I…I like it. Love it. Please don't stop."

Slowly, very slowly, Dale began to grind into him, his movements measured and steady. Zac's ecstatic moans encouraged him to move faster, harder, until his original urge was fulfilled, and he hammered home his desire again and again. He pushed one of Zac's legs off his shoulder then twisted him to one side. Zac gasped at the new position, his lips parted, and his fingers flexed.

"Yes!"

Dale renewed his rhythm. "You want to touch, don't you? Can you come without my hand, Zac?"

Zac yanked desperately on his chains. "Need…"

Dale kept moving. "I could stop. Leave you like this."

"Don't! Please don't!" Zac screamed, and his release fountained between them as if the threat alone had been enough to trigger his orgasm. His sobs were enough to make Dale lose control and he pumped his seed deep into the condom after a final drive. The crashing wave of Dale's release stole his breath. When it receded, he stayed where he was, allowing the aftershocks to roll through him. His arms trembled, and he locked his elbows. Zac's eyes were glazed, his expression one of blissed-out shock. Dale withdrew carefully, gripping the base of the condom. He nudged Zac's other leg off his shoulder before going to his knees.

"Don't move. I'll be right back." Zac's boneless sprawl suggested he wouldn't be shifting even if he weren't still shackled to the bed.

After a quick trip to the bathroom Dale returned to Zac's side. He looked completely stunned, hair falling into his eyes, the red marks of Dale's fingers outlined on the pale flesh of his narrow hips. Dale pulled the crushed pillows from beneath him and used a damp flannel to clean him up. Only then did he release his wrists, which bore multiple red indentations. He pulled the covers up and crawled in beside him. Zac immediately moved closer, resting his head on Dale's chest. Dale stroked Zac's hair, wondering at how soft the dark strands were.

"That was… I don't have the words. How do you feel?" Dale asked, his voice a little rough.

"I always hoped that my first time would be amazing," Zac murmured, "but that was incredible. I never dreamed that I would find someone who could make me feel the way you do." He shifted a little. "However, my ass feels like someone just shoved a red-hot poker up there."

Dale chuckled. "I did wonder if you might find me too hot to handle."

Zac turned and pinched a vulnerable nipple. "Don't flatter yourself! I can take anything you care to dish out."

"I see your inner brat has awoken. I love a challenge, Zac, and that's one I would be only too happy to respond to." Dale rolled over, imprisoning Zac beneath him. He gripped his arms hard and stole a bruising kiss. "Be careful what you wish for."

"I want everything with you. Everything you want to give me. All the stuff you talked about earlier, I want it all."

"Greedy boy." Dale kissed all the exposed skin he could reach. "Perhaps we should relocate to the dungeon for the next few days. You'll look spectacular in my chains."

"Yes, please." Zac nuzzled against him, puppy warm.

Dale couldn't stop smiling. Apparently wishes sometimes did come true.

Chapter Seventeen

"Where did Rayne go this morning?" Zac asked Tor as he and Dale made their way into the banqueting hall. "I don't want to him to miss my goodbye lunch."

Tor looked up from setting out cloth-covered baskets of bread. "He's out running an errand, but he'll be back in time, don't worry. You think Rayne would ever miss a slap-up lunch, especially when he hasn't had to do any of the work involved?"

"True, I guess." Zac grinned.

"Stop worrying about everyone else," Dale reprimanded. "Relax. This is the last time we'll all be together."

Zac reached for his hand. "I wish it didn't have to end. The last week and a bit has opened my eyes to so many things. I've enjoyed every moment, even the frustrating bits."

"I did enjoy locking you into that cock cage."

"A bit too much. I don't want us to be apart, Sir."

"I know and I'm going to miss you so much, but your father has plans for you, so we'll have to be patient. Rayne will take you to London, and you'll get to start your sightseeing."

"You could come to the hotel with me...stay until my bodyguard arrives."

"I have to get back to work too—unfortunately my business doesn't run itself. If I could stash you in the boot of my Mini and spirit you away, I would."

"I think that's what you were here to prevent, wasn't it?"

Dale grunted. "Do you think your father would look the other way if I kidnapped you?"

"Is it wrong that the idea of it is making me hard?" Zac whispered. "You could steal me away to your secret dungeon and keep me as your sex slave."

"That idea has way too much potential. You're leading me astray. If I came to the hotel, I'd never want to leave you. This way we get a clean break, and if I have my way it won't be for too long. As soon as time zones allow, I'm going to call your father, see how quickly we can be together again."

"I'll call him too. He's not unreasonable. It's a shame he can't meet you because if he did he'd know he could leave me in your hands."

"He's your dad. It's right he's cautious about your safety. I wouldn't want it any other way." Dale took his seat and took the time to admire the beautiful table settings. Someone, probably Skye, had put a lot of effort into the lush greenery, sparkling crystal and silver.

"Is it me, or are there too many place settings?" Dale muttered. "There are three extra, aren't there?"

Zac shrugged. "Maybe some of the regular staff are due back. The Retreat has new guests coming next week. Skye told me there's a big group arriving from the Netherlands." He hadn't let go of Dale's hand and seemed sad.

Tor bustled in and out, transporting bottles of wine and carafes of iced water. Dale didn't get the chance to ask him about the extra places. He concentrated on Zac, recognizing the anxiety bubbling beneath the wan smiles.

"I am really sorry we have to be apart. If I had my way, I'd never let you out of my sight again. We're still so new, and there are so many things I want to do to you."

"You mean *with* me."

"That too." Dale smirked.

"You're so bad!"

"Never thought I was good, did you? You said you liked rough around the edges. You'd need an industrial supply of sandpaper to smooth me down."

"You're perfect to me."

"Stop it, you'll make my head swell...and other things."

"Do we have time to go back to our room?"

"I'm afraid not. That cock cage is going back on at the first opportunity."

"So mean!"

Luke came into the room hand in hand with Skye, who was bouncing with excitement. "I love fancy meals! Doesn't everything look amazing, Sir?"

"Thanks to you." Luke gave Skye a long, lingering kiss that pushed a spike of envy into Dale's heart. Two weeks in Zac's company had been enough to convince him that they were meant to be together. It seemed so unfair that they had to be apart so soon. Zac's budding submission needed nurturing. He didn't need to be abandoned amidst a confusion of emotions and developing feelings. It was frustrating that Luke seemed entirely unconcerned as he and Skye took their places at the table. Dale held his tongue. He couldn't expect others to understand his simmering frustration.

"Here's Rayne," Zac said. "At least, I'm pretty sure I can hear a car."

"I think you're right." The crunch of tires on gravel preceded the clunk of car doors and low voices. "He's not alone." Dale caught Luke's eye and gave him a questioning glance. Luke's enigmatic smile only served to raise Dale's hackles.

As the new arrivals came inside and their voices got closer, Zac's eyes widened.

"Dad?"

It was Carey Hoffmann who came into the room first, closely followed by his sub, Alistair and Rayne. The fourth man Dale didn't recognize but from Zac's startled squeak and headlong run into the man's arms he guessed it was his father.

Dale glared at Luke. "What's going on, Luke?" Luke did his Mona Lisa impression and didn't answer.

Alistair made a beeline for Skye and soon the room was full of excited chatter. Luke tapped the rim of his glass and the hubbub quietened. He pushed his chair back. "Welcome, gentlemen. You're right on time." He smiled and walked across to shake hands with Carey.

"Everyone, let me introduce Taylor Denman, Zac's father," Carey said, glancing Dale's way. Zac detached himself from his father's hold.

"So this is him?" Taylor said, looking at Dale.

Dale wondered why Zac's father was heading directly for him. He glanced over his shoulder but there was no one else there that could be Taylor's target. Dale stood, shoving his chair back hard enough that it started to topple but he caught it just in time.

"Fast reactions. I'm pleased to meet you, Dale. I'm Taylor Denman." Taylor held out a hand, Dale shook it, bewildered.

"Why is it I get the feeling that I'm light years behind the rest of you?" Dale gave Luke a hard look, then Carey. Luke had the grace to appear sheepish, Carey just seemed smug. "You're far too pleased with yourself, Carey," Dale snapped. "What's going on?"

"I'd like to know too," Zac contributed.

"And me!" Skye piped up.

"Why don't we all sit down?" Luke suggested.

Dale remained standing until Zac returned to his side. They sat next to each other, and Zac slipped his hand into Dale's. Dale wasn't sure if it was because Zac needed support or if he was offering it, but the contact helped. Carey's relaxed attitude was irritating Dale no end. "Start talking Carey or you and I are going to have words."

Carey chuckled. "Of course. I'll keep this short. You all know that we arranged four Doms to meet Zac during his stay here. What you don't realize is that we actually arranged five."

Dale frowned. "I don't understand..." He took in Carey's grin and realization dawned. "Oh! You manipulative son of a bitch! Christ, I'm dumb as a box of rocks." He massaged his temples.

"Why? I don't get it." Zac squeezed his hand.

"The fifth Dom... It's me, isn't it?" Dale narrowed his eyes and debated wiping the smugness off Carey's handsome face.

Carey brushed an imaginary piece of lint from one pristine cuff. "Correct."

Skye gasped. "Did you know about this, Sir?" he asked Luke.

"I'm afraid so, love." Luke petted Skye's hair. "Forgive me?"

"Only if you tell me everything."

"I think Carey can carry on the story. I fully intend to blame him for all this." Luke gave Skye a chaste kiss on the cheek.

"Alistair is the guilty one. I'm afraid this was his idea," Carey said.

"Sir! That's not quite accurate," Alistair said, blushing. "I talked about Zac with my friend Olly…"

"Olly Dexter? Joe Dexter's husband?" Dale asked. "That explains a lot."

Alistair giggled. "You'll have to meet him one day, Zac, Olly is a legend. He suggested getting sneaky with a fifth Dom."

"Legendary brat," Carey muttered. "But on this occasion, the two of you cooked up a good plan."

"I'm still not following!" Zac exclaimed.

"When we were trying to decide which Doms might suit you Zac, we kept coming back to one man, Dale. But we didn't want you to meet in a structured way. We wanted you to find each other. With an occasional nudge in the right direction."

"Luke suggesting I work in the garden, for example?" Zac asked.

"Yes." Alistair nibbled his lower lip.

"And we had to concoct a reason to get Dale down here for the full two weeks so you could get to know each other. So I appealed to Dale's protective instincts," Carey said.

"The kidnap threat was never real then?" The start of a headache was forming behind Dale's eyes as he tried to keep up with Carey's devious manipulations.

"Not specifically," Taylor admitted. "Though Zac does have to be alert to the possibility."

"So when you spotted the drone," Carey said, "we didn't know what was going on. It was pure coincidence that young Aaron decided to get nosy at the exact same time Zac was staying here."

"You knew about all this too, Dad?" Zac gave his father an accusing glance.

"Carey came to me with the plan, and I thought it was a fine idea. Dale had glowing recommendations as a man and as a Dom. I was happy to endorse it."

"Unbelievable. What if we hadn't got our act together?"

"Then the four Doms would have visited as planned. You would have gotten your introduction to the lifestyle, Zac and possibly connected with one of them."

"Instead, I used my safe word because I only wanted Dale. Did the other Doms know what you were up to?"

"Not Marcus," Carey said. "At least not until just before he left. But Luke could already see that you and Dale had started to bond before Eric arrived, so we let him in on the secret. The others knew from the start that if things went to plan they might not be needed."

"So Eric knew exactly what he was doing in the dungeon that day?"

Luke nodded. "He did. We guessed you'd balk at more intense treatment from anyone other than Dale. Eric was prepared for your reaction. He came on strong in the hope that you would be brave enough to use your safe word."

"And I had to fly over to meet the man my son wants to be with," Taylor said.

"I should be furious," Dale said, "but your plotting brought me Zac, so I guess I can forgive you all. One day. Maybe."

Zac leaned against him. "This place has worked its magic again, hasn't it?"

"It should have worked it quicker, then Marcus wouldn't gotten his hands on you." Dale felt growly and unsettled.

"But if I hadn't been with him, I wouldn't have known what I needed or recognized it in you."

"Stop talking sense. It's disconcerting."

"You're crazy."

"Eric still got to see you naked."

"Dale, my father is listening to this conversation!"

"And he needs to know that you're off-limits to other men from now on. No more experimenting with the lifestyle. No more fixing you up with other Doms."

"Just you?"

"Just me."

"I think I get the message," Taylor said. "You were right about him, Carey."

Carey nodded. "Indeed." The unspoken 'obviously' had to be apparent to everyone in the room.

Dale sighed, wishing his brain was as sharp as Carey's. Tor, who had arrived halfway through the conversation, dressed in chef's whites, cleared his throat. "I have a kitchen full of food waiting for a celebration lunch, so if you've all finished yapping, perhaps you'd like to start eating?"

Skye snickered, and Luke gave him an indulgent smile.

"It is incredibly bad manners to keep such an accomplished chef waiting," Taylor said. "Zac sang your praises over email, Tor."

Tor inclined his head, accepting the compliment as his due.

"Go ahead, Tor," Luke said, rolling his eyes.

Tor grabbed Rayne, and within minutes the table was groaning under the weight of the feast they delivered. They also joined the group around the table.

"So you knew to expect visitors for lunch," Dale accused.

Tor shrugged. "I know better than to incriminate myself."

"He did." Rayne piped up. "He made special treats because Zac's dad was coming. Oh, I shouldn't have said that." He bowed his head over his starter, avoiding Tor's glare and the silent promise of spankings to come.

"I need to pay more attention to what's going on around me," Dale said.

"But your attention was on me, and I really enjoyed it." Zac snuck a sideways glance at his father, but Taylor was deep in conversation with Carey. "You know, I could put off whatever my dad has planned and come work for you until you can get some time off. Now my dad's here, I'm sure you could persuade him that I'd be safe with you. I can job hunt at the same time, but there's no rush for that. I want some time for us."

Dale stared at Zac, hardly daring to hope that what Zac had suggested might be a possibility. "You'd do that? You were really looking forward to seeing all the gardens you've been researching, and he's bound to have made arrangements for security."

"I don't have to do them all at once, though, do I? We could visit gradually, together. You could come over to the States and spend some time in Arizona too." Zac sounded so hopeful, Dale couldn't bear the thought of letting him down.

"Don't get your hopes up yet. Enjoy the meal then we'll talk to your father afterwards when we have a bit more privacy, okay?"

For the rest of lunch, Dale's thoughts were in a whirl. He had resigned himself to being apart from Zac for a while, but it was the last thing he wanted. Zac needed his Dom. Dale needed his sub just as much. His feelings had deepened over days alternating between the dungeon and peaceful walks in the grounds, bondage and laughter. Their moods always seemed to match. When Zac craved deep submission, Dale made him fly. When Dale was more contemplative, Zac took pleasure in serving him. For the first time in his life as a Dom, Dale enjoyed after-care as much as an intense scene. He wanted to continue the journey he and Zac had begun and see where it took them.

Once the meal was over and coffee served, Alistair and Skye wandered off arm in arm, chattering away, while Luke muttered something about having work to do. Tor dragged Rayne in the direction of the kitchen leaving Dale, Zac, Taylor and Carey at the table.

"So where will the two of you be heading next?" Taylor's guileless question surprised Dale so much he gaped.

"Dad! You mean it? It's okay for me to go with Dale?" Zac was vibrating with excitement.

"If he can put up with you — where else would you be going?"

"He can! He so can. He doesn't let me get away with anything but I...we thought you'd have other plans."

"I'm not so stupid as to get between a Dom and his sub. Plans can be changed and this situation was always going to be fluid."

Dale shook his head. "I'm an ordinary working man, Mr. Denman. I can't offer Zac the kind of lifestyle he's been used to. I want him with me more than anything but I'm a realist—we're from different worlds."

"Taylor, please." Taylor held up a hand to silence Zac's protests. "There's nothing ordinary about you, Dale. If you've stolen Zac's heart, then what more does he need? He's a grown man and it's time he made his own way in the world. An over-protective Dom will keep a closer eye on him than I ever could, short of locking him up at home and making him miserable. He knows his own mind and believe me, the lifestyle you're talking about is not one that Zac is especially attached to."

"What about his security? I won't put him at risk."

"If you'll allow it, I would like to assist with upgrading any precautions you have at home, but I don't want Zac living in fear. A little anonymity will be good for him. No more attending social events that you hate, Zac."

"Thank God," Zac mumbled. "If I never have to put on a dinner jacket again, I won't complain."

"If you're working with me, you'll be lucky to get out of a pair of overalls," Dale said, drily. "Are you sure about this? We've only known each other a very short while."

"All the more reason we should spend more time together. I have so much to learn."

"That's settled then." Taylor made a grab for the coffee pot. "I need to stave off jet lag and this coffee is fantastic."

"What are your plans while you're in England, Taylor?" Carey asked.

"Some very dull meetings in London then on to the Far East for my annual round of hand shaking to keep my customers happy."

"Rather you than me, Dad." Zac bubbled with happiness, a beaming smile fixed to his face.

"I think you're going to have your hands full, Dale."

"Don't worry, I can handle him just fine."

"From what I've heard, I don't doubt it." Taylor gave a happy moan as he drank more of Tor's coffee. "We'll talk more and stay in touch while I'm traveling."

"And if I need anything…?" Zac began.

"You'll come to me," Dale said firmly.

"What he said," Taylor agreed, sending Dale an understanding look.

Dale relaxed, knowing that Taylor would support him in his role as Zac's Dom. The future had become much brighter, and Dale couldn't wait to bring Zac fully into his life.

Epilogue

Two months later…

"I love you, Zac." In Dale's head each word sounded distinct, they were carved on his heart, etched into his brain. Giving them life always lifted weight from his shoulders and set something free inside him. He didn't say them enough.

Zac, whose gaze had been fixed to the floor, lifted his head. "What did you say?"

"I said I love you. Pay attention."

Soft green eyes gazed at him, testing how serious he was. He stared right back, unblinking, safe in the knowledge that he would win this little game. He always did. Zac's shoulders dropped, and he pulled his thin black sweater over his head. Even now, undressing in front of Dale as part of a scene brought a flush to Zac's cheeks and his cock obediently to attention. Dale loved Zac's unstudied reactions and hoped he would never change. He still had an innate innocence, expressing wonder at every new experience.

Zac unbuckled his belt and slid it through the loops of his waistband. He rolled it into a neat spiral and placed it on the arm of the chair in front of Dale's fingers, which he was now tapping impatiently, sending Zac a signal not to dally. Hurriedly Zac unbuttoned his jeans and slid them off. He was wearing his favorite underwear — low-rise black Calvin Klein trunks that hugged the contours of his body closely. Dale appreciated the choice — they were becoming his favorites too. They were already damp, the stretchy fabric resisting Zac's erection so that when he pulled them down his cock sprang free with a bounce. The diamond bead of moisture that had gathered at his tip seemed to float momentarily in the air before dropping on a length of spider silk moisture to the floor.

"You're eager. I like that." Dale gave Zac's cock a light flick then picked up the belt. The leather was still warm. Zac had assumed a display position, legs apart and hands clasped behind his head. He'd become so much more graceful in his submission over their months together, more contained somehow. Dale gave a brief nod of satisfaction. He got up then circled Zac, admiring the lines of his lean body, even more honed now from hard work. Dale had shaved him the previous evening, leaving Zac's groin bare. Dale stroked the bared skin. "We'll make this permanent, I think. A new rule." He relished the dynamic of being fully clothed when Zac was naked, the shaving accentuated Zac's vulnerability even more.

"I...yes, Sir."

Dale stopped behind Zac, leaned in close and blew warm breath onto his neck. "Are you ready to play, love?" Dale ran his fingers down the side of Zac's neck then followed the line of his arm to his wrist. Zac shuddered as Dale nudged him to bring his arms down until his hands were clasped behind his back, resting against his ass. Dale continued the delicate tracing touches, interspersing them with kisses that barely brushed Zac's skin.

"Please, Sir…"

"Hush, sweetheart. Begging isn't going to get you anywhere, you know that."

"But…"

"Should I gag you?" Zac shook his head. "Then be good. No talking unless it's to use your safe word."

Dale threaded the belt through its buckle then placed the resulting loop around Zac's wrists, slowly cinching it tight. He threaded the free end of the leather between Zac's arms a couple of times. The binding was snug, taut enough that Zac would be aware of the leather against his skin but unknotted so that he could get loose if he wished to. He showed no sign of wanting to be released—quite the opposite. Zac always seemed to relax once he was in bondage.

Dale stroked the swell of Zac's ass, lingering at the point where soft flesh met firm thigh. His cock was rigid, straining and when Dale snaked a hand between Zac's legs to grasp his balls an anguished cry escaped his lips.

"There now, I've got you." Dale encircled Zac's waist with one arm, holding him tightly, while he continued to torment him, squeezing Zac's balls to a point that Dale judged to be just shy of pain. Then he let go. He repositioned Zac so there was a gap between them, enough space that he could rub a finger between Zac's ass cheeks.

"So much heat. Don't move or you lose even the remotest chance of coming." Dale had to release his hold in order to reach for the lube. He coated his fingers then, without warning, plunged two inside Zac's channel, scissoring them as wide as he could. Zac ground his ass back against Dale and Dale responded by driving his fingers in as deep as they would go. He fingered Zac roughly, enjoying his needy whimpers and cries of pleasure. With his fingers still buried deep, Dale reached around Zac's body to grasp his cock and one swift tug was all it took to push him over the edge. Zac came hard, tugging desperately at his bonds.

"Stop struggling, boy. You know better." Dale probed at Zac's prostate over and over, milking him dry until Zac sagged into his arms, and Dale's fingers slipped free. Swiftly, Dale untied Zac's wrists, pulled his arms in front of him and retied the belt. "I'm not done with you yet. On the floor."

Panting, Zac collapsed to his knees, and Dale shoved him forward onto all fours, though his bound wrists meant that he had to rest his forearms horizontally on the carpet. His ass was pushed high into the air, and Dale's pulse pounded at the sight.

"Stunning." He paused for a few seconds, giving Zac a chance to use his safe word if he needed to. Not that it was likely. Over the last two months, Dale had learned that Zac loved to play rough. Since they'd been together, the only time Zac had used his safe word was when he'd been in restrictive bondage and developed a maddening itch on his nose. Dale chuckled at the memory. Clever knotting had allowed him to release Zac in seconds, and he'd rolled on the floor, scratching his nose and moaning in pleasure.

"You're remembering that itch, aren't you?" Zac mumbled.

"Might be."

"You're never going to let me forget that, are you?"

"Quiet, or I'll gag you with something uncomfortable. And no, it had far too much entertainment value. I was going to fuck you, but because you're incapable of keeping quiet, I think I'll give that gorgeous ass a few stripes first."

Dale's small but select collection of paddles, crops and canes was stored in a suitcase under the bed. He pulled it out, ignoring Zac's accusing gaze. In a moment of indecision he hovered between a flexible cane and a rubber coated paddle. The cane won. A few experimental practice flicks made a satisfying whistle as they cut the air. Dale rolled his shoulders then turned his attention to Zac's behind.

"The marks fade so quickly," he mused before laying a stroke diagonally across Zac's flesh. "Much better."

"Ow!" Belying his yell, Zac waggled his butt. He loved the sharp burn of the cane.

Dale gave him two more firm strikes, creating a gratifying pattern of crossed lines. Zac groaned, already hard again. "Still making so much noise." Dale hid his smile and stripped his clothes off before going to his knees, straddling Zac's legs. He positioned his cock at Zac's entrance, happy that he no longer had to deal with slippery condoms. He grasped Zac's hips, took a deep breath and rammed into him. Zac was so slick from the earlier fingering that Dale sank in to the hilt in one smooth thrust. Zac whimpered at the invasion and the sound spurred Dale on. He dug his fingers into Zac's narrow hips and pounded his beautiful ass like it was the last chance he would ever have. It was only after he had shot his seed deep into Zac's body that he registered Zac's sobs.

"Oh God, Zac." Dale pulled Zac him into a hug, "I'm so sorry!" He waited for Zac to speak, expecting to be pushed away at any moment. Slim hands cupped his face, then soft lips met his own. Zac's wrists were still bound but he didn't seem to notice.

"Sorry for what, you daft idiot?"

Dale was confused. "You were crying, I hurt you."

"If you were on the receiving end of that battering ram of yours, your eyes would be watering too!" Zac grinned.

"So you're okay? I thought I might have missed your safe word, I got so carried away."

Zac ducked his head then nuzzled Dale's shoulder. "I love it when you get rough, you know that. Does that make me a freak?"

"It makes you adorable." Dale untied Zac's hands. "You could have gotten free any time you know."

"I know." Zac's smile said it all. He knew exactly what turned Dale on too.

"Don't think I missed you calling me an idiot, by the way." He led Zac over to the bed.

"You have ears like a bat. No way would you ever miss my safe word, you doofus. Sir."

"Doofus? You are feeling brave." Dale ushered Zac beneath the covers.

"I need cuddles."

"You need another spanking."

"I don't!"

"You definitely do. I think you'll appreciate a long-haul flight all the more with a warm behind and a chastity device."

"I'd set off the metal detectors!"

"They come in acrylic, you know."

"Oh."

Dale chuckled, and Zac cuddled closer.

"I love you so much," Zac murmured.

"What brought that on?"

"Well, you said it earlier and I didn't, so…"

"That was part of the scene. I don't need you to tell me how you feel, I know."

"You might not need it, but I'm gonna tell you over and over…till we're old and gray."

Dale rubbed a hand over his short-cropped hair. "You won't be able to tell when I go gray."

"Why don't you grow your hair?"

"Because I have blond curls and look like a choir boy," Dale said.

"Oh my God, really?" Zac shook with laughter. "What I wouldn't give to see that. I should call your mother and tell her to get the albums out."

Dale reached beneath the covers and gave Zac's cock a sharp flick.

"Hey!"

"A sore behind, a cock cage and a plug. A nice fat one." Dale gave a happy sigh of satisfaction. "Life is good. Arizona sunshine instead of miserable British weather to look forward to and a naughty sub to punish. What could be better?"

"Uh, no punishment?" Zac placed a few kisses on Dale's neck.

"I'm happy for you to keep trying to convince me to be lenient," Dale said.

"But it never works!" Zac complained. "If I'm walking funny when we arrive, my dad…"

"Will shake my hand and congratulate me on keeping you in line."

"He will, dammit. It's a conspiracy."

Dale gave Zac's ass a light slap. "Are you sore?"

"Nope. Sticky, though."

"Then we may as well get dirtier before we get clean."

"Is that a request or an order, Sir?"

"Definitely an order."

Zac flopped onto his back. "This is what a happy ever after feels like, isn't it?"

Dale chuckled. "Give me a minute and it'll be an even happier ever after, love."

Want to see more from this author? Here's a taster for you to enjoy!

Treasure Trove Antiques: The Gilded Mirror
L.M. Somerton

Excerpt

"Moving apartments involves way too much physical exertion." Landry Carran launched two garbage bags full of bed linen into the spare bedroom before continuing to the kitchen to survey the chaos. "I'm exhausted and I have bruises in unmentionable places. Why aren't cardboard boxes spherical? Corners are evil."

"You're moving one floor down in the same building." Gage Roskam, Landry's boyfriend, poked his head around the door. "And you have half of Seattle PD's finest helping out, so quit whining or I'll spank you in full view of all of them."

"That'd scare the uniform pants off 'em. Something I wouldn't mind seeing one little bit." Landry contemplated the idea of a bunch of semi-naked cops with delight.

"Not so much. I've heard at least three different people say you need a spanking today. None of them seemed bothered about when or where it happened."

"I'm offended!"

"You're a brat."

"I just want boxes marked 'kitchen' to go in the kitchen. Do they not teach reading at the police academy?"

"Not so's you'd notice."

"I never knew I had so much stuff," Landry muttered. "It's like living in one of those anxiety dreams where you know you have to finish something but it's never-ending." He shuddered.

"Are you one of those hoarder types? I think full disclosure should have occurred before I agreed to move in with you, if that's the case." Gage shoved another box of kitchenware onto the already crowded counter.

"You've been living with me for almost six months. You invaded my closet, kept your toothbrush in my bathroom and installed a gun safe in the bedroom. You discovered my rubber ducky fetish, stole an entire box of peanut butter cups and left your huge-ass boots where I'd trip over them. Just because you kept paying rent on your place does not mean we weren't living together."

Gage shrugged. "Your rubber fetish is a lot broader than ducks." His blue eyes twinkled.

"That's where you're going with this?" Landry pouted. "Stop grinning."

"Come here." Gage crooked his finger.

"Nope." Landry folded his arms. "Not gonna."

Gage blinked. "Right now, Landry."

"Or what?"

"Hmm, let me think. There's that new latex hood with the built-in penis gag—that has possibilities. Chastity for the next week—always fun—or removal of coffee privileges."

Landry decided the three steps into Gage's arms were his best option. He rested his cheek on Gage's chest. "So mean."

"And you love it."

"Not admitting to anything that might prejudice my defense. Ooh, you're so warm and you smell good."

"How can that be when I've been carting boxes and furniture all day?"

"Don't know, don't care, but it's true and that T-shirt shows off your muscles so well. Very distracting. You reduce my productivity." Landry stroked a firm bicep.

"Oh no. You are not prepping the ground for blaming me when you can't find your favorite mug this evening, or if some random object goes missing. Your productivity would increase if you spent less time drinking coffee and more time hauling shit. Less gossiping with Sancha needs to go on that list, too."

"I don't know what you mean." Landry made his eyes big and wide and projected innocent vibes.

"My box of toys is in our bedroom. I have several paddles you haven't met yet. Tonight, you'll pick one then count while I apply it to your ass." Landry gulped and his cock jerked. Gage snuck his hand down the front of Landry's pants to give his shaft a squeeze. "Someone wants that spanking real bad."

"Not me."

"This says different." Gage played a little more. "You're leaking."

"Unhand me, you brute."

"Have you been watching old British films again?"

"Maybe." Landry shoved his groin into Gage's palm.

"*Madre de dios*, put that boy down!" Sancha Hernandez, Gage's partner, shouted from the hallway.

"Or at least wait until I have a better view. There's unpacking to do, and I was promised beer and pizza for helping out. I've seen no evidence of either and as I *am* a detective, I'd know."

Landry whimpered as Gage gave him a final squeeze before removing his hand from Landry's pants. "Later, brat." Gage grabbed his cell from the counter. "I'll order the pies before we have a mutiny on our hands. You sort the drinks. I'm not unpacking anything else tonight. The bed's made. I have a toothbrush. I'm set."

"I can't believe you're leaving me all alone for three whole days," Sancha moaned, joining them. "Who's gonna buy my coffee and fill in my paperwork?" Landry sniggered. "I can't believe the captain signed off on your vacation time. Do you have blackmail material on him I don't know about?"

"Pretty sure you'll survive by enlisting some other naïve sucker," Gage muttered before putting in his pizza order.

"Junior detectives are meant to make themselves useful. I'm giving them valuable life experiences and don't forget my garlic prawns," Sancha prompted him.

"And that right there is why I'm glad I don't have to share a car with you tomorrow," Gage said. "There aren't enough air fresheners in the world."

Sancha shrugged. "Lightweight. How are you doing, Landry, sweetie? I hope you haven't been carrying anything too heavy. Moving is hard work, and you need to stay hydrated. Why don't you grab a soda then come sit with me?"

"That sounds so cool. I *am* a little achy." Landry directed his pout at Sancha.

"I'll be on the couch." She smiled at Landry, scowled at Gage then left the kitchen.

"Why doesn't she care if I've been overdoing it?" Gage complained. "I'm the one she spends every day with."

"Duh. Because you have muscles on your muscles whereas I'm a delicate flower."

"Who shifts furniture around all day in an antique store."

"Details. This much cuteness needs to be protected." Landry swept a hand down his body.

"Yes, I'm still here. Sorry. Someone delusional was interrupting me." Gage finished ordering food while Landry got himself a soda. He turned from the fridge to find Gage looming over him. "You give me a crick in the neck when you do that." Landry tilted his head back. "I need a stool or a box or something."

"I think my partner loves you more than me." Gage twisted his fingers through Landry's hair.

"I'm a lovable person. Of course I'm Sancha's favorite. She loves me best because I am way cuter and far more adorable than you. You have this whole broody, menacing thing going on." Landry grinned. "Which is a huge turn on for me, gotta say."

"I know."

"You do, huh?"

"I do."

"I should go talk to Sancha…"

"You should stay right here while I remind you who you belong to."

Landry drew breath to speak but his words were cut off as Gage captured his lips in a demanding kiss. Every submissive gene in Landry's body responded to Gage's dominance. He moaned into the kiss, knees wobbling. Every tug Gage gave his hair sent a miniature bolt of lightning to Landry's cock. When they finally parted, he took a step back, dazed.

"I...that was...wow."

"Now you may go and talk to Sancha."

"Oh I may, may I?" Landry hesitated, wondering if he might get kissed into silence if he talked back. "You don't get to tell me who I can and can't talk to." Gage gave him one of his patented 'don't mess with me' looks. "Okay, sometimes you do. Not all the time, 'cause I'm a grown-up and I make decisions for myself. Like when we have cookies, and I have to choose between chocolate chip and ginger. I can do that."

"No you can't. You always take both."

"Bad example." Landry scuffed the toe of his sneaker on the floor.

"I know you're all grown up, sweetheart, and you're quite capable of making decisions. Mr. Lao wouldn't trust you with Treasure Trove if you weren't. But you're mine and that gives me a say in your life. Sometimes you need a nudge in the right direction is all."

"And that's your job?"

"Along with watching out for you, tying you up, fucking you into the mattress, protecting you from predatory British art thieves..."

"You had to go there."

Gage smirked. "Go keep Sancha company. I'll go wait for the pizza guy and let the others know food is on the way. I think pretty much everything that needs to be, has been moved."

"Bring them all in here, yeah? There's a cooler full of beer behind the couch—unless Sancha has already found it, in which case it may be half-full by now." Landry ambled through to the sitting room, which had a similar layout to the one in his old apartment except for an extra nook for a dining table. He threw himself onto the couch where Sancha was glugging down a bottle of Dubbel Entendre, which Landry had sourced from Sound Brewery in Poulsbo.

"You found the cooler then." Landry leaned into Sancha's side.

"I can scent beer from a mile away, you poor innocent lamb. Of course I found it and damn, this beer is good. Just what I needed. Love the name of this stuff too."

"I couldn't resist it, it's such a cool name." He cracked open his soda. "Thanks for helping out today, I really appreciate it. I know you don't get much free time, and you must have had better things to do than helping me and Gage move."

"How many times have you guys helped us out? Besides, it was this or taking the kids to soccer practice. My loving husband saw fit to remind me that I tend to get over-excited around the coach who I happen to think would have a much more lucrative career as an underwear model. Honestly, he's wasted on a bunch of kids."

"Leering in front of children is not a good plan." Landry slurped his drink.

"Sad but true. However, we're not here to talk about my perversions."

"We're not here to talk about mine, either," Landry cautioned. "Because that would take way too long."

Sancha gave an unladylike snort. "Ain't that the truth? Also, Gage might object. So, tell me what Mr. Lao is up to and why you get to move into his apartment. Gage is hopeless at filling me in. I need to get the details from you. Mr. Lao isn't ill or anything, is he? I kinda like the old guy."

"He's fine. More than fine. He's moving in with his girlfriend."

"He's... Run that by me again."

"He has a girlfriend called Maisie. He met her at his seniors bowling club – that's bowling on grass by the way, not bowling on an alley, and now they're moving in together in some gated community in the 'burbs, complete with health club, tennis courts and on-site restaurant. He's stepping back from the store, to spend more time with her – semi-retirement, I suppose you could call it. I get to be the store manager and one of the perks is to move into Mr. Lao's old apartment, which as you can see has more square footage than mine. The kitchen is bigger and there's a spare bedroom, which is great because I can hide all Gage's junk in there."

"Congratulations! Manager, huh? Does that mean you get a humongous raise?"

"I wish. I agreed to a percentage of the profits on everything I sell on top of my puny salary, plus this place which, despite the lingering scent of incense, is quite a perk. Mr. Lao will still be doing most of the buying while I get to park my butt in the store. He loves traveling around finding great deals and bartering with his pals in the trade. Oh, I also get to look for an assistant. A new me."

"And Gage is moving in with you. That's so sweet."

"I dare you to use the word sweet in front of him. It's practical. He saves a bundle on rent, and I get to jump his bones any time I want. We were as good as living together already, anyway."

"More like he gets to keep a closer eye on you."

"Exactly," Gage said, joining them. "Because someone has a habit of getting into strife when I'm not watching him." He dropped a pile of pizza boxes on the coffee table and the room was soon swarming with all the people who'd been helping out with the move. The noise level and banter grew as the pizza mountain shrank and the beers from the cooler were drunk. Landry laughed at all the jokes Gage's colleagues made about him, noticing that they were a lot more cautious about teasing Sancha. When he mentioned it, she laughed.

"They wouldn't dare. The last time one of them tried to play a trick on me at the precinct, I accidentally stapled his hand."

Landry looked to Gage for confirmation. He nodded. "She did. Not sure it was accidental, though."

"No comment!" Sancha proclaimed.

"Your aim is spot on, and you know it!"

"And on that note, I think it's time that me and this crowd of reprobates cleared out of here and left you two lovebirds alone."

Landry fought back a yawn. "You don't have to go yet."

"It's been a long, hard day and you're going to be really busy with setting up this place until the store reopens on Monday. Take the peace and quiet while you can and besides, Gage is needy. You have to keep stroking his...ego." She snorted with laughter before levering herself off the couch. She gave Gage a kiss on the nose then began ushering everyone out of the apartment.

"Give me a minute," Gage said. "I need to make sure they've really gone."

Landry giggled. He curled into the corner of the couch and nibbled on a leftover slice of pizza. A wave of fatigue washed over him. He'd been so excited about the move, he'd been up since dawn and hadn't slept much the previous night. Snuggling in bed with Gage sounded like a fine way to end the day, even if the bed was still surrounded by boxes.

By the time Gage returned, Landry was half-asleep.

"You have drool coming out of your mouth." Gage's graveled tones pulled Landry from his doze. He rubbed at his mouth with the back of his hand. "So this is how it's going to be. One day living together, and you're already letting yourself go."

"If I had the energy, I'd swat you for that remark," Landry muttered, yawning.

"You look like you're about to go into hibernation."

"That's not a bad idea. Did you know there's a Twitter account that follows a bunch of bears in Alaska and people get to vote on which of them is the fattest before they hibernate. These guys are chonks, let me tell you. They get to eat whatever the hell they like, pile on the weight then snooze away the cold months and when they wake up, they're all skinny. Mind you, I'm not that fond of salmon. I don't think bears eat pizza."

Gage gaped. "I worry about you."

"I know you do. Makes me all gooey inside thinking about it."

"Sometimes I wonder how you survived before you met me."

"I managed just fine." Landry squeaked as Gage scooped him into his arms.

"That's not what your brothers tell me."

"You are way too close to those Viking wannabes and you shouldn't believe a word they say about what I did or didn't get up to as a child. They lie."

"They have photographic evidence."

"Image editing software is a thing, you know. It's all fake, whatever they say." Landry pouted as Gage hauled him into the bedroom. Gage dropped him, and he landed on the bed in a sprawl.

"Get your clothes off, brat." Gage's feral expression sent shivers down Landry's spine. He scrambled out of his clothes with indecent haste, full of renewed energy. "Sure you're not too tired for this?" Gage removed his T-shirt far too slowly for Landry.

"Don't tease me, Gage! And no, I'm not too tired. Raring to go." Landry licked his lips at the sight of Gage's chest. "Your bare skin has magical energy powers."

"Hands and knees." In his rush to get into the position Gage wanted, Landry got too close to the edge of the bed. Gage caught him as he toppled off the side. "Don't want you bruising your backside before I get to it." He manhandled Landry back onto the bed.

"My hero." Landry batted his lashes. He got onto his hands and knees, wiggling his ass in blatant provocation. His cock, hard and aching, bounced. He was hot, feverish with anticipation and when the smack of leather against skin sounded in his ears, he jumped.

"Just testing it against my palm."

Landry twisted, trying to get a look at what 'it' was. The paddle Gage held was rectangular with a tapered end, the handle a snug fit in Gage's hand. "Oh…"

"I was going to let you choose but decided you were too tired to think straight. This is double-layered leather, hand stitched and reinforced with a metal plate."

"I don't need the technical specification, Gage."

"Sir."

"Feeling especially Dommy are you…Sir?" With a happy sigh, Landry rested his head on his folded arms, widened his legs and wiggled his butt a bit more.

"I should gag you." The paddle connected with Landry's backside with a thwack. He moaned. "But then I wouldn't get to hear the noises you make." Gage delivered a further four blows before dropping the paddle on the bed. Landry forced himself to take slow, even breaths while heat, edged with pain, blossomed across his skin. He was desperate to come and on the edge of begging Gage to fuck him. When Gage stroked Landry's sore skin, he whimpered.

"So pink and pretty. You want me in you, don't you? You want me to stuff you full." Landry couldn't summon enough coherence to respond, and when Gage pushed a cool, lubed finger into his ass, Landry sobbed. "So needy. Sucking me in."

Landry worked Gage's finger with his inner muscles, muttering nonsense words under his breath. Gage added a second finger, then a third in quick succession, stretching Landry's channel enough that it burned. "Pl...pl...platypus!" Landry refused to beg. Gage enjoyed it far too much.

"Is that a new safe word?" Gage withdrew his fingers.

"No!" Landry wailed. "Put them back!"

Gage flicked Landry's balls. "What's the plural of platypus?"

"I. Don't. Care."

"I should get my phone and check or perhaps we could find the box with the dictionary in."

Landry sobbed. "I hate you."

"No you don't." When the blunt head of Gage's cock made contact with his pucker, Landry sucked in his breath. "Relax." Gage moved at a leisurely pace.

"I've seen pregnant hippos move faster than you." Landry yelped as Gage reached around his body to pinch a nipple.

"That spanking wasn't punishment enough, was it?" Gage pushed home, then stilled. "I need to think of better disincentives."

"That's a hellishly big word considering what you're supposed to be doing," Landry muttered, trying in vain to push back onto Gage's cock.

"Quiet, brat, or tomorrow you'll be unpacking with a vibrating plug stuck up your rear." Gage took hold of Landry's hips and pounded his ass with unbridled enthusiasm. All Landry could do was brace himself and take it, and that suited him just fine. Now Gage was doing exactly what Landry wanted him to, Landry could relax and enjoy the rush of pleasure, the surge of orgasm, as it flooded through him. When Gage came, he dug his fingers into Landry's hips, yanking him back so that he was as deeply impaled as it was possible to be. He could have come untouched, but it was Gage's firm grip on his cock that tipped him over the edge. Landry cried out, spilling into Gage's hand in a series of uncoordinated jerks before collapsing face down on the bed. For a while, Gage let his weight rest along the length of Landry's body. Landry loved being held down, loved being rendered helpless by a bigger, stronger man. Gage knew it and took full advantage, sinking his teeth into Landry's shoulder.

"Wanna mark me, huh?" Gage didn't bother confirming or denying. He sucked at Landry's skin. "What do you call a hickey surrounded by teeth marks?" Landry wondered.

"I call it mine."

Landry gave a happy sigh. "No one will see it under my shirt."

"I'll know it's there and that's all that matters. Tomorrow, your ass will ache, your shoulder will ache and every twinge will make you think of me."

"I have other things in my head apart from you, you know."

"In that case…" Gage rolled to one side then flipped Landry onto his back. He hooked Landry's legs over his arms, bending him back. "I'd better fuck you again because those other things need to take second place to me."

"You talk a good game, Sir, but there's no way you're hard again yet."

"I don't recall saying what I was going to fuck you with, and by the way, you doubting my powers of recuperation focuses my mind even more on how best to punish you."

"I should be quiet now."

"No, by all means carry on. That hole you're standing in can still get deeper." Gage groped beneath the covers and extracted a sizable dildo.

"You are a virile, masterful Dominant, Sir. I can think up some more positive adjectives, but I need a minute. You're distracting me with that…thing."

Gage grinned. "Nice try. You need more lube?"

"No? Wait, if I say yes does that buy me some time?"

"What do you think?" Gage touched the tip of the toy to Landry's hole then pushed.

About the Author

Lucinda lives in a small village in the English countryside, surrounded by rolling hills, cows and sheep. She started writing to fill time between jobs and is now firmly and unashamedly addicted.

She loves the English weather, especially the rain, and adores a thunderstorm. She loves good food, warm company and a crackling fire. She's fascinated by the psychology of relationships, especially between men, and her stories contain some subtle (and some not so subtle) leanings towards BDSM.

L.M. Somerton loves to hear from readers. You can find her contact information, website details and author profile page at https://www.pride-publishing.com

PUBLISHING

Sign up for our newsletter and find out about all our romance book releases, eBook sales and promotions, sneak peeks and FREE romance books!